WATER AND BLOOD

WATER AND BLOOD

STORIES

JULIE ANN STEWART

DZANC
BOOKS

DZANC
BOOKS

2580 Craig Rd.
Ann Arbor, MI 48103
www.dzancbooks.org

Library of Congress Cataloguing-in-Publication Data available upon request.

ISBN: 9781950539437
First US edition: April 2022
Interior design by Michelle Dotter
Cover design by Matt Revert

"By a Thread." Poemmemoirstory. January 2016. Print.
"9/12." Punch Drunk Press. 27 September 2017. Online.
"Show Me." Tishman Review. April 2017. Print.
"Liberty." LitroUSA. November 2019. Online.
"Baptism." Good River Review. March 2021.Online

Printed in the United States of America

10   9   8   7   6   5   4   3   2   1

To Rachel Elizabeth Ann, as promised.
May you always remain half savage and hardy, and free.

CONTENTS

"The blood of the battlefield is thicker than the water of the womb."
—Proverb

BAPTISM

I watched my sister Laura drown in the Ohio River.

The river pulled her into its embrace, enveloping her until its water kissed her lips. Not clear spring water, tipped from a glass. This had a smell of earth to it.

When the water rose above her mouth, Laura panicked. I saw it in her eyes. When it filled her nose, she tossed her head back, delaying what she knew was coming. The water stroked the back of her neck, briefly touching her hairline and then the top of her head. She flung her arms and thrashed her legs but she could not make all her parts work together to save herself, and so in a moment, her hands were the only part left in the air and she was grasping for something, the way she must have reached up when her mother laid her down in the cradle and she remembered wailing to be picked up, pushing open her mouth below the surface, the water filling her and capturing the sound of her cry.

And then, in answer, she was entombed in water, as she had been in the womb, but having forgotten how to survive there. And she was sinking, the water pouring in like soup and she was the ladle.

•

That was the last time I entered the water until today.

•

When we were postulants at the Mother House, many girls grieved the loss of childhood pleasures. They spoke of swimming in pools and creeks and backyard ponds, the way other girls pined for the old beaus they did not marry.

I liked to bathe quickly, often asking one of my sisters to wash my hair in the sink, preferring water poured over me to that in which I must submerge myself. I say a blessing that I was born Catholic, baptized as an infant, Holy Water sprinkled on my head while my godmother held me in her arms.

Clinging to the overturned boat, I had watched my sister Laura, on her twenty-second birthday, reach out to me. She had been thrown into the water with the rest of us. She flung herself around like a fish at the end of a line. Then her head, her nose, her arms, her hands, her fingertips slipped below the surface. At the funeral, there was no body, just a closed casket with a framed photo on top and twenty-two white roses. I was eleven, turning twelve the day of the visitation, our birthdays only two days apart, two days and ten years Mother would add. I wore my new dress, too festive, but the only one that fit, as I had grown an inch every month that year. Had it only been two days before that I was wearing that dress, sitting beside Laura as she practiced for her first solo violin performance?

Has it truly been over thirty years since she drowned?

•

During the school year, I teach at Our Lady of Providence in St. Louis, but during the summer, I return to the Motherhouse, as do most of my sisters. One year I was assigned to work in the sewing room. I found it difficult to imagine that I was doing the work of our Lord, of Jesus, who baptizes us with eternal life, while my hands pieced together those garments that only, barely, covered a woman's torso. After my first day, I walked straight to the confessional.

The fabric was like nothing I had worked with before. I had to remove the seam on the first garment I sewed three times before the fabric laid flat. It was thick and heavy, like the wool of my first vestments, but with a give to it. I could pull it the width of my arms and yet it returned to its original shape when I let go.

Before dawn each morning, I heard the other sisters giggling in the hall on their way to the pool. I wondered if one of them might be wearing a suit I have sewn. One morning, I rose and dressed and rode my bicycle across campus. Behind the gymnasium, I let the bike fall to the ground and pushed my face against the wavy glass windows, the way neighborhood boys had done, my brother's friends, trying to peer beneath the curtains on Saturdays when all of us girls bathed before mass.

Cupping my hands to block the sun, I saw blurs of color, dark navy shapes that were the swimsuits I had sewn, fleshy peach lines that were legs and arms, a backdrop of jeweled aqua blue, so different from the dark, muddy water of the Ohio River.

I heard His voice, telling me not to be afraid.

From thirty years before, I heard another voice too, that of Ernie, my sister Laura's fiancé. They would have been married the following spring, when an early Easter meant they could hold the ceremony while the forsythia was blooming.

"Don't be afraid," Ernie had said to her, holding her hand as she stepped from the dock into the boat rocking between us.

I was already seated, at Ernie's urging, to encourage Laura to be brave. A wink and a smile from him was all I needed to be convinced to play along. Ernie was the first man, the only man, I ever knew who was kind and tender and funny, who didn't yell after a few beers. I was young, I know that now, even if I have never loved another man besides Him, but even Mother liked Ernie, so different from Father and my brother.

He never married, Ernie.

The paper got his name all wrong. Who would name their son Urban? It was my fault. After the storm, things were so chaotic and the wind was howling at us and Ernie did not have time for the newspaper man who wanted to get the story, so I spoke to him, between my crying and looking over at Ernie's kneeling form, who was still hoping the doctor would be able to revive Laura.

We knew she could not be saved. She had been in the water too long.

River water is different from what I saw behind the thick panes of glass. The river was anger where this was peace, a laughing peace judging by the peals of laughter ringing out from the sisters. It echoed inside the chamber.

The river was dirty and had tried to pull me under too. This water was clean and bright and buoyed them along stroke after stroke until they reached the other side then it turned them around to go again. None of them wanted to escape this body of water. They craved it, drank it in through their skin.

This water called to me, offered to wash away the past, cleanse and caress me.

By then the light was rising outside, so I climbed back onto my bicycle and rode to the dormitory. I went through my regular routine: prayers, celebration of the Eucharist, breakfast, chores. But at work that day, I began cutting the navy and white fabric for one more bathing suit.

•

It was agony waiting to request permission to swim from the Mother. She had no reason to refuse, but would she ask me why?

Mother Theodore and I had been novices together. She was my superior then, even though she had stayed behind while I went out into the world to teach. Still, I remembered the day we sat side by side to cut off our hair, both of us looking down in apparent humility, but I, at least, was watching our shorn hairs, hers and mine, mingle together on the floor.

Now, sitting across from her, I was looking down again. She, I knew, was looking right at me.

"Many of the younger sisters are enjoying exercise in the water. You would be the first of our generation to join, Sister Marie."

"I know," I said, keeping my head down.

"Are you certain you will be comfortable with it?"

I looked up, wondering how she knew about the accident.

"I believe the attire has kept many of us away. It has been so long since I wore anything but my habits," she says, smiling. "You should have seen the first outfits approved by the bishop. We might as well have jumped in a river and drowned ourselves as try to float in those skirts."

I searched her face for cruelty buried in the remark, but there was only her smile. She did not know about the current that threatened to carry me away.

Tears rose at the inside corners of my eyes. I quickly looked back down.

"Sister Marie? I apologize. I did not mean to upset you. Are you sure you are all right?"

"Yes, Mother. Just tired. I have not been sleeping well."

"The exercise will do you good. If you are not an experienced swimmer, or need some assistance after so many years out of the water, Sister Mary John has been called to lifeguard for us. She will watch over you."

I knew no one could promise to keep me safe, but I thanked Mother Theodore and excused myself to wash up before dinner. I felt filthy after a day in the sewing room, the heat of the machines and July's humidity. At the porcelain sink in my room, I cupped my hands, let the water gather there, overflow the sides, run down to my elbows, even drip onto my dark habit. I tried to imagine water all around me, covering my head and nose and mouth. Fear rose in my throat like vomit, threatening to dredge up my lunch. The new suit hung on a hook beside my nightgown—two snapshots of one woman taken years apart.

.

The next morning, I rose with the bells. Like a child in winter, I pulled my arms inside the sleeves of my nightdress. In the dark, I pushed the gown up over my shoulders. I reached for the bathing suit and stepped one foot and then the other through the leg holes, wishing for the protection of the long skirts Mother Theodore spoke of.

You might as well have jumped in a river and drowned yourself.

I had never spoken to anyone about what I had witnessed. I was rescued from the water and watched as my parents were told that Laura was not. No one grieved for me, only looked to me for comfort.

"Did she die peacefully?"

"Was she frightened?"

Torturing me with questions to which we all knew the answers, avoiding the one they wanted to ask.

Why didn't someone save her?

I know now what they meant, all of them, my parents and Ernie and my brother. Why didn't I save her? I understand; my parents wanted their daughter back. I don't believe they would have preferred to have saved her and lost me instead, but rather, they knew I could take care of myself. Laura was someone that needed protecting. They knew Laura had to be convinced to get into that boat, by Ernie, and by me, the adventurous one, the tree climber, the rope swinger, the bicycle rider.

I know they thought I ran away to the convent to hide.

Maybe I wanted to find a way to save someone else, in her place. If my strong legs had not saved my sister, they could run the length of a kickball field at recess. My arms had not reached for her, but they could hug, even discipline a child, especially one who got neither at home. My mind failed to devise a plan to rescue her, but it could teach my class how to reason through a math problem and decipher a word and learn any number of skills necessary to survive, to thrive.

I struggled to pull the suit up over my hips. The thick double-knit scaled my thighs then inched up my body. The skin covering my legs was nearly as white as my nightdress. It almost glowed. I wrestled it over my backside and up to my waist. I put my arms through the wide straps, pushed my gown over my head and dropped it to the floor. My breasts fell into the padded cups that I had sewed into the lining. The neckline had a small scoop that revealed the dip at the base of my throat. I felt naked touching the skin there, knowing it would be exposed. I shuddered as if I had a chill. It did not help to think of the other sisters dressed identically. I called to mind an image of prisoners, how the sameness of clothing didn't remove the shame.

I hung my gown on the hook and slipped my day dress over my head, let the skirt fall into place. Without stockings, the hem brushed my bare calves. Our skirts had already grown shorter over the years. I didn't know it them, but it would not be long before we sisters stopped wearing headpieces altogether, before we were granted permission to return to our birth names, although most of us older ones kept our religious names. We didn't know ourselves as anyone else anymore. We had no desire to go back to being the person we used to be.

I slipped my bare feet into solid black shoes.

There is no going back. Even after we face our fears, do the thing we have avoided. We are changed, new, reborn into something else, something unfamiliar. Therein rests the fear. Who are we without our guilt, our regret that things turned out the way they did? Why do we hold onto it for dear life, when in fact it is a brick that weighs us down?

I heard the sisters in the hall then. I opened my door. They looked at me but showed no surprise. They nodded, out of respect. I was older than all of them by at least a decade, perhaps more. I walked behind them, thinking I could be invisible, but this made them more self-conscious, believing I was witness to every step, every turn of their heads. They did not know that I walked with my head down.

At the front door, we stepped outside. Heat rushed at us. The temperature was already nearly eighty. We walked silently, following the brick path across the lawn. Sunlight filtered through the trees. I jumped when a single brown leaf fluttered down on my left, so gracefully that as first I thought it was a bird come to light on my shoulder. I brushed the leaf away and kept walking, skipping a bit to keep up. Occasionally I had to take an extra step out of time not to get left behind.

When we reached the pool house, it looked like it was on fire. The rising sun reflected its light off the glass roof. I put my hand to my forehead and squinted to see. We filed in, each person holding the door until the sister behind her had lifted her hand to hold it open for herself. I was last. I heard the latch softly click behind me. The floor was tiled in blue and green, without any obvious pattern, as if someone kept reaching into a box and pulling out one and then another without a plan. Blue, then green and green and green again, blue then green, until finally the finished floor reveals a pleasing array, beauty in the chaos.

In the changing room, we slipped off our dresses and hung them up. We were all the same pale white beneath, even those who had been swimming the longest.

When I sat at the edge and slipped my feet into the water, I knew it was nothing like the angry water that took my sister. This water was calm and cool, as beautiful as it looked from outside. I wanted to let my whole self slide in, but something held me back, a tether. Maybe it was the one that kept me alive.

I could have reached out to Laura that day on the river. I chose to hold on. There were ten of us in that boat and not one person, not even Ernie, let go to save her. After they fished out her body, a doctor spent three hours trying to revive her, to make up for our lack of courage. He must have known it was hopeless. No one comes back to life after being gone so long. Why did he keep trying? For Ernie, or my parents? For me?

Perhaps he did it for himself, to save himself, to say he had done all he could.

•

We can drown ourselves in fear and guilt.

Or we can let go, let it be washed away like dirt after a long day's work.

•

I would like to tell you that I dove into the pool that day and let it all go. I did not. I sat there at the edge, my feet making rings that rippled outward until they reached the other swimmers.

Every morning that summer, I rose and pulled on my navy suit. I walked to the water's edge and sat down, dipping my feet, my calves.

•

Not until today do I let myself slide in, let my hips and stomach and breasts and head, my arms—flung over my head—then my elbows and wrists and hands and each fingertip go under the water.

As I come back up for air, I think, how easy it is rise to the surface.

CONFESSION

IN 1920, WOMEN IN THE US earned the right to vote, and the Ku Klux Klan sent David Curtis Stephenson to Evansville. In 1922, the year my aunt drowned in the Ohio River, he moved to Indianapolis to make the Indiana Klavern one of the most powerful in the nation. I have heard it said that if a man was white and Protestant in Indiana at that time, he belonged to the Klan.

Five years later, a jury of a dozen men—ten farmers, one truck driver, and a businessman—would find him guilty of the rape and murder of Madge Oberholtzer. He went to prison, was released on parole, arrested several years later for sexually assaulting a teenage girl, sent back to prison and released again. He moved to Tennessee and married a third time. He died in 1966, the year I was born in a Daughters of Charity hospital in Evansville.

My parents named me after the nun who ran the hospital. Sister Juliana.

Now I live in an old neighborhood in Indianapolis, ten blocks from the home where D. C. Stephenson lured Madge late on a Sunday night.

She walked to his house from her own family home, forgetting her hat and ignoring her mother's warning. She would be returned two days later by Stephenson's bodyguard (a former police officer from Evansville). She died in the bed she'd slept in every night of her life save the previous two. A childhood friend of my daughter lives in the house now. Has my daughter slept in the room where Madge lay?

Before her death, Madge gave a statement that would provide the basis for Stephenson's conviction.

I, Madge Oberholtzer, being in full possession of my mental faculties and conscious that I
am about to die, make as my dying declaration the
following statements:

My name is Madge Oberholtzer. I am a resident
of Marion County, State of Indiana, residing at
No. 5802 University Avenue, Indianapolis. I first
met D. C. Stephenson at the banquet given for the
Governor at the Athletic Club early in January,
1925.

After the banquet he asked me for a date several times, but I gave him no definite answer. He
later insisted that I take dinner with him at the
Washington Hotel and I consented and he came for
me at my home in his Cadillac car, and on this oc-
casion we dined together.

They know me there, at the Washington. They had a table ready for me, or perhaps they knew better than to put me off. The table was robed in white. A single candle flame flickered in the center. Its light reflected off of the crystal goblets and shining silverware. Madge noticed these things and commented that it looked very pretty. The waiter brought us steaks, porterhouse, rare. When I cut into the tender flesh, blood ran out and pooled at the edges of the white china plate.

I asked my dad if he remembers the KKK in Evansville when he was young. He told me he remembers crosses on front yards and Black families' houses being burned to the ground. He remembers marches by the big fountain downtown, the one built for farmers to water their horses. He remembers men dressed up as nuns, pretending to have sex with each other. He remembers the names of the three Black families that lived in his neighborhood—the Watsons, the Larkins, and the Poseys. (Mr. Posey was a preacher, he said.) The other families were all German immigrants.

This was the first time I had heard that the KKK targeted German Catholics and immigrants. There weren't enough Black people up north yet to encourage folks to join the Klan. So the leaders focused their efforts on immigrants and Catholics and Jews. They talked of purity of the Anglo-Saxon race, the "Nordics," they called themselves. They narrowed the definition of what it meant to be white. They took out ads in the newspapers and held picnics and got a hold of lists of people who belonged to Masonic temples. Protestant ministers became their mouthpieces, touting Prohibition and drunkenness and the need to protect their women, keep them pure.

Stephenson bribed many politicians in the state, including the governor and senators. He forced them to introduce legislation that would close all parochial schools. He wanted to make it illegal for nuns and Catholics to teach in public schools as well.

After that he called me several times on the phone, and once again I had dinner with him at the Washington Hotel with another party.

I wanted to introduce her around. I wanted her to meet the people who knew me, so they could know her. She worked for the Education Department. I thought she could help me write the textbooks I wanted to sell to the public schools when I got the new laws passed. I was going to marry her. She would be Mrs. Stephenson; I would keep her safe, protect her purity. But when she realized who my colleagues were, who I was, the light went out of her eyes. After that, she stopped taking my calls.

On a warm fall afternoon, I set out to walk to Madge's house, a charming Foursquare on a corner lot with a deep front yard. A curving footpath snaked from the street to the porch steps and a front door with stained glass windows on either side of it. I tried to imagine Stephenson's bodyguard carrying her limp body up the wooden steps. Did the screen door creak when he opened it? Did he prop it open with his foot while he tried the lock or did he knock? Did she have the strength to turn the knob herself?

Inside, Madge directed him up the stairway to her room. He laid her on the bed and left, retracing his way out the front door and down the steps and the curving path to the sidewalk and the waiting Cadillac.

I stood there for a while on a cracked square of sidewalk. It had buckled, and it rocked unsteadily beneath me. I remembered a day that my daughter's friend's dad got angry and yanked her out of the car by her arm and tossed her on the lawn. I remember the look on her face, looking up at him, blinking her eyes but not saying a word, not even crying. And I remember my daughter too, chin dropped, mouth open, staring. I think the girls were six or seven at the time.

I did not see him again until Sunday, March 15, 1925, when upon returning to my home about ten o'clock in the evening I was informed by my mother, who said to me that there had been parties calling for me on the telephone and saying for me to call Irvington 0492. I called Irvington 0492 and Stephenson answered and said

come down if you can to my home,
I wish to see you about something very important to me
I am leaving for Chicago and have to see you before I leave.

This was about 10 p.m. Sunday.

His home was only two or three blocks from mine. He said further

I am busy and cannot leave, but I will send someone for you.

Soon a Mr. Gentry, whom I had never seen before, came for me and said he was from Stephenson's. I walked with Gentry to Stephenson's home.

I walked alone with Madge on my mind, westward, from her home to his. I admired the old houses—their turrets, porches, light glinting off the old hand-rolled glass windows. I crossed the street and walked through the grassy park in the center of Audubon Circle where a fountain bubbled. In my time, the twenty-first century, this park is a place to sit in Santa's sleigh on luminary night, where local bands play concerts on summer evenings, the street barricaded while children race around and around on bikes. Dads and moms look on from the grassy area, sipping from plastic cups of wine or beer. In October, neighbors gather to hear scary stories from an actor dressed as Edgar Allen Poe. He recites "The Raven" and "Lenore" and finally, in its entirety, "The Legend of Sleepy Hollow" while a black horse clip-clops over the old bricks, a headless rider carrying a glowing pumpkin in his lap.

Today the circle is quiet. The sun is up. I stop to dip my fingers in the water of the fountain. The lid to a trash can is turned upside down in the water, and I see an open book beneath the water's slightly green surface. And then I remember something I had read: Madge left her house in such a hurry, urged by Stephenson and then the man who showed up to escort her, that she had forgotten her hat. What would her mother say, a proper young lady going to a see a man at his house late at night, without being properly dressed?

```
When we arrived there we went inside. I saw
Stephenson and that he had been drinking. His
chauffeur, whom he called Shorty, was there also.
Shorty is a young man. Later a man whom they called
Klenck came in. Soon as I got inside the house
    I was very much afraid
    There was no other woman about
    Stephenson's housekeeper was away
    They took me into the kitchen.
    Some kind of drinks were produced
    Clenck came in the back door
    Stephenson and the others forced me to drink.
    This made me very ill and dazed and I vomited
```

all over the fucking floor. It splattered my shoes. I'd sent the house-keeper away, so I yelled at Clenck to get a fucking rag to clean it off. I couldn't go on the train like that. That is when I first saw fear on her face. I wanted to make her understand that it was okay. I would protect her.

```
Stephenson said to me about this time, "I want
you to go with me to Chicago." I remember saying I
could not and would not. I was very much terrified
and did not know what to do. I said to him that I
wanted to go home. He said,
```

No, you cannot go home. Oh, yes! You are going with me to Chicago. I love you more than any woman I have ever known.

I tried to call my home on the phone but could get no answer. Later when I tried to get to a phone they would not let me. These men were all about me. They took me up to Stephenson's room, and he opened a dresser drawer which was filled with revolvers. He told each of the men to take one, and he selected a pearl-handled revolver for himself and had Shorty load it. Stephenson said first to me that we were going to drive through to Chicago. He said for me to go with him, but I said I did not wish to and would not go to Chicago. Later Gentry called the Washington Hotel, at Stephenson's order, and secured reservation in a drawing room for two persons. They all took me to the automobile at the rear of Stephenson's yard and we started the trip. I thought we were bound for Chicago but did not know. I begged of them to drive past my home so I could get my hat, and once inside my home I thought I would be safe from them.

Stephenson does not take her home.

He drives on to the train station. They go in one of his Cadillacs; he owned four. The garage where he kept them is still there at the back of the large lot, behind the white house with white columns and a white picket fence, like hooded men guarding his castle. In Indiana, he was a big fish in a small pond.

I am the law in Indiana.

He had been denied national leadership by the Imperial Wizard of the Klan and sent here and he had done well for himself. He owned factories that produced the white robes and hoods, and for every new member sworn in, he earned several dollars in profit. The robes were designed to exact specifications that prevented men from having wives sew their robes at home. Stephenson used his millionaire fortune to pay for the renovation to a simple Queen Anne house in a quiet suburb in Indianapolis and built the long garage out back that housed his four Cadillacs. He was important. He had the governor and the senators in his pocket. Everyone did his bidding.

We got on the train, and although I cannot distinctly remember, I think only the colored porter saw us. They took me at once into the compartment. I cannot remember clearly everything that happened after that. I know Gentry got into the top berth of the compartment. Stephenson took hold of the bottom of my dress and pulled it up over my head. I tried to fight but was weak and unsteady. Stephenson took hold of my two hands and held them. I had not the strength to move. What I had drunk was affecting me. Stephenson took all my clothes off and pushed me into the lower berth. After the train had started, Stephenson got in with me and attacked me. He held me so I could not move. I did not know and do not remember all that happened. He chewed me all over my body, bit my neck and face, chewing my tongue, chewed my breasts until they bled, my back, my legs, my ankles, and mutilated me all over my body.

Afterwards Gentry and Stephenson helped me dress and the two men dressed and they took me off the train at Hammond. I remember seeing the conductor. I was able to walk to the Indiana Hotel. I remember begging Stephenson and saying to him to wire my mother during the night and he said he had or would, I am not clear about that. At the Indiana Hotel, Stephenson registered for himself and wife. I tried to see under what name but failed to do so. This was about six thirty in the morning. There were in the hotel lobby two colored bellboys and two colored girls. Gentry, Stephenson went to the rooms. I had no money. I kept begging Stephenson and saying to him to send my mother a telegram. I said to the bellboy, "Are there any blanks in the room?" Stephenson made me write the telegram and said to me what to say. Gentry took the telegram and said he would send it right away. Stephenson lay down on the bed and slept. Gentry put hot towels and hazel on my head and bathed my body to relieve my suffering. We were in room 416 with Stephenson while Gentry was doing this. Stephenson said he was sorry, and that he was three degrees less than a brute. I said to him, "You are worse than that." Breakfast was served in the room. Shorty came in about this time. He said he had driven up in Stephenson's car. Stephenson ate grapefruit, coffee, sausage, and buttered toast for breakfast. I drank some coffee but ate nothing.

They do have a good breakfast at the Indiana Hotel. I stop in Hammond often on my way north. I remember being ravenous that morning and that hearty breakfast put me in good spirits. When she asked for $15 *to buy a hat, I told Shorty to get it for her from my breast pocket. I didn't want to stain my suit jacket with grease. I told him to drive her to the shops, let her get what she needed. I stayed in the room and finished eating. We had to get to Chicago for a business meeting."*

I went into a store close to the hotel to get a hat, a small black silk hat similar to one I have—it cost $12.50. I said to Shorty, drive me to a drugstore in order I might get some rouge. I purchased a box of bichloride of mercury tablets. I put these in my coat pocket.

Earlier in the morning I had taken Stephenson's revolver. I wanted to kill myself then in Stephenson's presence. Then I decided to try and get poison and take it in order to save my mother from disgrace. Later, after I had taken the mercury tablets, I lay down on the bed and became very ill. Then Shorty came in. He said to me what was wrong that I looked so ill.

I replied, "Nothing." He said, "Where is your pain?" and I said it was all over. He said I could not have pain without cause.

When I said to him I had taken poison he turned pale. He then went out. Stephenson and Gentry and Shorty came into the room very much excited.

Stephenson said,

What have you done? I ordered a quart milk and made her drink it.

I said to Stephenson, "What are you going to do?" And he said,

We will take you to a hospital here and you can register as my wife.
Your stomach will have to be pumped out.

He said to me that I could tell them at the
hospital I had gotten the mercury tablets through
mistake instead of aspirin.
I refused to do this as his wife.
Stephenson said,

The best way out of it was for us to drive to Crown Point and get
married.

Gentry said he agreed with him. I refused. Stephenson snapped his fingers and said to Shorty,

Pack the grips.

Stephenson helped me downstairs. Just before we
left, Hammond I said to Shorty to call my mother up.
He said, "If I do that she will be right up here."

That would have been a disaster.

And I said, "What could be sweeter." Stephenson
said to me he had called her. I said to him, "What
did she say?" And he replied that she said it would
be all right if I did not come home that night.

When I read Madge's statement the first time, I had never heard
the term "pack the grips." I assumed it meant pack the guns. I looked
it up online. Turns out a grip is an old-fashioned term for a suit-

case. Madge was dying, her body covered with bite wounds, bleeding through her dress. She was vomiting blood from ingesting mercury poison. Still Stephenson takes time to pack their suitcases. I'm not sure why, but this detail sticks with me.

I cannot grasp how a man, after assaulting a woman, is able to wake from a good night's sleep, eat a breakfast of eggs and sausage and toast with jam, hand the woman $15 to buy a hat and (unbeknownst to him) mercury poison, discover that she is dying, and insist that his butler pack their bags so they can drive to Crown Point to get married, seeping wounds staining what would be her wedding dress while she carries not a bouquet but a bowl for bloody spittle.

We women are weary of these stories. They re-traumatize, over and over and over. We weep. We eat. We drink. We reach out to strangers. All to numb us to the truth that in this country, people would rather ignore a bleeding, traumatized woman than acknowledge that we have put our trust in a monster. We tell our truths and then the world—our families, our leaders, the American people—go on as if nothing has happened.

Men: Rape a woman. Pack the suitcases. Do a business deal. Arrange a marriage. Make a movie. Win an Oscar. Get elected to Congress. Get elected governor. Get elected to the White House. Get appointed to the Supreme Court.

Women: Get raped. Poison yourself. Try not to bring shame to your mother. Try not to ram into the red Dodge Ram truck with a *Trump that Bitch* bumper sticker. Get diagnosed with fibromyalgia and lupus. Have a hysterectomy. Take a small white pill every night before you go to bed. Go to church and say the Our Father every Sunday. Sit on the bathroom floor cutting your arms with a pair of your mother's sewing scissors. Put a shot of vodka in your Diet Pepsi before going to work. Marry a man who assumes that if you don't want to have sex with him, you must be getting laid by someone else. Have an affair. Leave your husband. Go back to school to become a writer. Tell your story. Beg the man's butler to take you home, which he does, carrying you upstairs and laying you in your childhood bed, where you die two weeks later from a staph infection that originates at the bite wound on your breasts. But not before you make your statement about what he did to you.

I don't know much about what happened after that. My mind was in a daze. I was in terrible agony. Shorty checked out for all of us, and they put me in the back seat of the machine with Stephenson. We then started for home in the automobile. After we got a piece Stephenson said to Shorty to take the auto license plates off of the car, which he did, and Stephenson said to him to say if questioned that we had parked in the last town we had passed through and auto plates had been stolen. All the way back to Indianapolis I suffered great pain and agony and screamed for a doctor. I said I wanted a hypodermic to ease the pain, but they refused to stop. I begged and said to Stephenson to leave me along the road someplace, that someone would stop and take care of me if he wouldn't. I said to him that I felt he was crueler to me than he had been the night before. He said he would stop at the next town before we got there but never did. Just before reaching a town he would say to Shorty, "Drive fast but don't get pinched." I vomited in the car all over the back seat and grips.

Stephenson did not try to make me comfortable in any way. He said he thought I was dying, and at one time said to Gentry, "This takes guts to do this, Gentry. She is dying." I heard him say also that he had been in a worse mess than this before and got out of it. Stephenson and Gentry drank liquor during the entire trip. I remember Stephenson having said that he had power and saying that he had made $250,000. He said that his word was law. After reaching Indianapolis, we drove straight to his house, cutting across Emerson Avenue or 38th Street some way. When we reached Stephenson's garage he said, "There is someone at the front door of the house." It was sometime during the night when we got to the garage, as I think we left Hammond about five o'clock, and Stephenson said to Shorty to go and see who was at the front door. Shorty came back and said, "It's her mother." I remember Stephenson said to me, "You will stay right here until you marry me."

Stephenson, or someone, carried me up the stairs into a loft above the garage. Stephenson did nothing to relieve my pain. I do not remember anything that happened all night, after we reached the garage. I was left in the garage until I was carried home. A big man, the Mr. Clenck mentioned before, took me home. He shook me and awakened me and said, "You have to go home." I asked him where Stephenson was and he said he did not know. I remember Stephenson had told me to tell everyone that I had been in an automobile accident, and he said, "You must forget this, what is done has been done, I am the law and the power." He said to me several times that his word was the law. I was suffering and in such agony I begged and said to Clenck to take me home in the Cadillac car. He said he would order a taxi, but finally said he would take me in Stephenson's car. He put my clothes on me and then carried me down to the car and put me in the back seat and drove the car to my home. I said to him to drive up in the driveway. He did and then carried me into the house and upstairs and into my bed. It was about noon Tuesday when we got into the house.

I, Madge Oberholtzer, am in full possession of all my mental faculties and understand what I am saying. The foregoing statements have been read to me and I have made them as my statements and they are all true. I am sure that I will not recover from this illness, and I believe that death is very near to me, and I have made all of the foregoing statements as my dying declaration and they are true.

MADGE OBERHOLTZER

Madge died a few days after making her final statement. Stephenson was found guilty, though he never confessed to the crime of rape and murder. From prison, he continued to write the governor, expecting to be pardoned. When that did not happen, D. C. offered information that led to the indictment of the governor and other leaders who had accepted Klan bribes in exchange for favors.

•

I recently attended a lecture offered by a local historical guild about the Klan, D. C Stephenson, and the rape of Madge Oberholtzer.

The talk was held in an old classroom at the defunct state mental hospital. Rows were terraced up to a high ceiling that gave me a feeling of vertigo as I climbed the steps to find a seat. Around me hung paintings of old white men, presumably the respected doctors on the forefront of medicine in the early twentieth century. I was uncomfortable having them look down on me. The room filled up, and the speaker stepped to the podium. I don't remember his name, and by the end of the lecture, I would be too upset to ask.

He opened by thanking the museum for inviting him. He was an older white man, dressed in slacks and a navy-blue dress coat, a white handkerchief neatly folded in the breast pocket, a retired dentist. He sipped from a Styrofoam cup with a white plastic straw. He had a white bushy mustache that rested on his upper lip.

He said there were three heroes to this story. He named three men.

He added that the victim was Madge Oberholtzer.

He went on in a jovial tone. He made fun of the Klan language, of Kludds and Klecktokens and Klorans. He flipped the pages of his speech with a flourish. He performed a show, part drama, part comedy routine.

When he finished, people in the audience began to ask questions which he struggled to answer.

Afterward, a group of four women, myself included, stood by the podium talking to him. One of the women was a nurse. She wanted to clarify his suggestion that the poison Madge took was used to induce abortions. When the woman said that Madge's autopsy showed she had taken in the poison orally not vaginally, the lecturer furrowed his white brows and said:

You know what I've always wondered? $12.50 sounds like way too much money to spend on a hat.

We all looked at him.

One woman said, well, hats were an important fashion accessory for a young woman at that time, particularly one who made her own money.

And how did they force her to drink whiskey? You can't force someone to drink.

Another woman said, they had guns.

I said, she was alone with three men.

He threw up his hands.

I guess. I'm not saying she wasn't telling the truth. It just doesn't sound right to me.

We looked at him and at each other. There was nothing else to say.

The man took a sip from the white straw of his Styrofoam cup. His wife was waiting and impatient to get going.

I have questions too.

Madge, why are you buried in a Masonic cemetery, a cemetery that created a separate location for people of color?

Did you know that Klan leaders used Mason membership lists to recruit new members?

What were you doing at a party celebrating the inauguration of Governor Ed Jackson, Klan member, later indicted for bribery, the man D. C. Stephenson counted on for a pardon?

What he did to you was awful.

But, Madge, I wonder, what were you before you were a victim?

BY A THREAD

The first time I call the Domestic Abuse Hotline, pretending to be concerned about a neighbor lady, the volunteer on the other end tells me that the worst thing to do is tell her to leave Him.

"Why?" I ask.

"Abusers take away your identity."

She doesn't mean *my* identity. She means the more general *you*, like when Julia Child says, then you take your chicken and place it ever so gently in the pan, breast side up.

"An abused woman sees herself as he sees her. She cannot imagine surviving without him telling her who she is."

After I hang up the phone, I sit on the floor, next to my bucket of mop water, and weep.

This is the day I start to record my life, so I can see myself, our first day in this new house, dragging along His promises to fix things up. I go through the boxes and dig out the movie camera we received when Isaac was born. I set it on the kitchen table under the window, press the button that makes the little red light come on, and go back to cleaning the kitchen. When I clean, I lose myself completely. The smell of bleach calms my nerves, burns my nostrils and keeps me feeling safe, as if a perfectly clean floor gives us a fresh start too. .
After I finishe the video of me scrubbing the floor, I move on to

the baseboards and the walls. I carry the camera into each rooms with me, so that by the end of the day, I have footage of me washing dishes, wiping down the banister, making beds and dusting the shelves onto which we will unpack the books.

I want to see myself from a point of view other than His. I think maybe I can help the woman I had become save herself.

•

Isaac laughs and sing-speaks, "Four and twenty blackbirds, baked in a pie."

"Not blackbirds. Black*berries*," I correct, laughing with him.

Isaac Nolan Stephenson, as his birth certificate reads, is my son. It took us days to settle on a name, until finally, the nurse came in my room and said if we wanted to be discharged, we had better decide what to call our little boy. In fact, I found out later we could have left him unnamed for up to a year. That's what the other moms at the preschool told me, the same women who were appalled when they found out we had Isaac circumcised. It is strange how vulnerable we are. I had been so certain of myself before the birth, and here I was, only a few days later, being bullied into names and medical procedures.

It's not that I disliked the name Isaac. I just wasn't as sure of it as He was. I was sure I wanted to breastfeed. I was sure I wanted to have John Denver music playing in the delivery room. I was sure I wanted my first meal after he was born to be vanilla ice cream, the good kind with dark flecks of seeds.

After I was settled in my room, He brought chocolate ice cream from the cafeteria.

"I wanted vanilla," I said, trying not to sound disappointed.

"Chocolate tastes better."

"To you maybe, but not to me."

"Well, it's too late now. I already got it."

I ate the chocolate. How long before that became my favorite flavor? Now it is the only kind in the freezer. I remember that I bought it for Isaac's first birthday, when my whole family came to stay with us.

Looking back, I wonder if anything about life is our choice. As sure as I was about vanilla ice cream, that's how sure I was that I wanted a baby, that I was ready to be a mother. What He made me believe is that someone gets to decide what your name is and what your body will look like for the rest of your life, like they are casting you in a role that they chose for you. You act; they direct.

And so, Isaac Nolan Stephenson it was.

"Isaac, hand me that rolling pin."

The pie is for my husband. He works at a salvage yard, tearing down old barns and outbuildings on farms that are being turned into subdivisions and strip malls, taking the parts and turning them into expensive, impractical things that are sold in galleries and high-end shops.

"What about worm pie, Mommy? Can we make that?"

"You mean like the dirt pie we had on your birthday?"

"No, worm pie, with real worms, like the ones that come up out of the ground when it rains."

All boy, I thought, but I did not say it. "Sure, Isaac. Let me get my pie in the oven, and then we'll get yours started."

Chances are good that he will forget that promise and become interested in something else by the time we finish my pie. If not, what harm will there be in digging up a few worms, getting muddy, stomping in puddles? Those kinds of messes can be cleaned up.

Isaac circles the kitchen island while I roll out the crust, turning back to the stovetop to stir the cooling berries, then back to smooth the crust, crimp the edges into ruffles. I pour the contents of the pot over the pastry. Isaac comes round my side of the island as I am bisecting the pie with the first strip of lattice crust.

"Uh-oh, Mommy. You spilled."

I look down at my feet. Bright purple splatters, like a Rorschach blot, on His freshly laid white tile floor. It had missed my foot by less than an inch.

"I'm glad it didn't land on your pretty toenails, Mommy. That would have burned you 'cause it's hot, right?"

"That's right, Sweetie," I say, though I would have taken that pain instead.

"Hot like what's in a witch's pot, huh?"

"Yes, that's right."

"Boil, boil, toil and trouble, is that right? Mommy?"

"Yes," I said. "That's right."

I set the pot back on the burner, careful not to drip anymore, though a few bruised berries cling to the sides. I grab a thick yellow sponge from the sink and kneel down to wipe up the mess. The inky mixture shifts from floor to sponge, but a purple stain stays put.

Tossing the sponge back into the sink, I open the cabinet and pull out a spray bottle of cleaner with bleach.

Bleach can clean up any mess, I thought, even blood.

Isaac continues to circle the island, widening his arc around me and the fresh stain. I spritz cleaner onto the tile and watch it settle into the grout, using the bottom corner of my old stained apron to blot at it.

The dark lines remain, maybe even grew brighter.

"I'll let it soak for a few minutes," I say out loud, to myself. Isaac has enlarged his circle into the dining room and is coming back to make a full figure eight. I unscrew the cap, lift the spray nozzle from the bottle, and pour a thin stream of cleaner onto the floor. It puddles, bubbles forming at its edges, and then seeps in. "What if I can't get the stain up?"

The phone jangles.

"Honey, let it go," I call to Isaac.

But he already has it in his hands, putting it up to his ear and mouth.

"Hello?"

I can hear His cheery voice.

"Hi, Daddy. Guess what? Me and Mommy and are making worm pie!"

He sounds impressed, then asks if I am there.

"Yes, she can talk. She is cleaning up a little mess."

Isaac delivers the phone to where I kneel beside the sink.

"Hello?"

"You aren't really making worm pie, I hope."

"Of course not," I said. "Blackberry. Your favorite."

"Okay. Good. He has an imagination, that kid. And some-times…you know."

"Don't worry," I tell Him, running my fingers across the slick-ened blue spot.

"Okay. I'll be home in an hour. I'm knocking off a little early, so I can seal that kitchen tile before dinner."

"Today?"

"Gotta get it done before anything ruins it."

I stare into the black spot, which stares back without flinching.

"Babe, you there?"

"I'm here," I say. "I better get going, though, if I'm going to be out of the way when you get here."

"That's my girl."

I end the call. My knee has started to shake now, bumping the cabinet door against the frame with a clat-clat-clat, tapping out a message in Morse code.

If He has not yet sealed the floor, then the stain is permanent.

Nothing can get rid of it, no amount of bleach or scrubbing. I have cleaned the whole house, mopped every floor, dusted the furniture and the baseboards, made the beds, vacuumed and swept and polished, except in the kitchen, which I had saved for last, until after I slid the pie into the oven.

Now, all that is left is damage control.

First, I have to get Isaac down for his nap. He has plopped himself onto the couch to watch cartoons. The sound is turned down; figures run and chase and punch each other in silence. His eyelids are heavy as he fights off sleep.

"Isaac, let's get you to bed, and when you wake up, we can dig for worms."

I scoop up his small body, binding him to me, the way mothers do: one arm over his legs, the other under his torso with a hand resting on his back. His legs have gotten so long this summer. His feet dangle past my limbs instead of curling around my body the way they did when he was small. We walk up the carpeted steps. When I lay him down, he cries out, for just a moment or two, before he closes his eyes and pulls himself into a fetal position.

When I stand up, I see the video camera on top of his bureau, from when I had last recorded myself. I pick it up, turn it so I can look into the little screen at the back, rewind it until I view a miniature version of myself, rocking Isaac to sleep, turning sideways in the chair to keep the pressure off of my bruised ribs. The small woman sits rocking and rocking, too small for me to make out if she is still crying, but if she is, it too was silent, like Isaac's muted cartoons. The camera has not filmed what happened in our bedroom, Him shoving me out of bed, telling me to find another place to sleep.

I turn off the camera and set it gently back on the shelf.

•

The afternoon sun is shining through the windows when I hear His boots crunching across the driveway gravel. Twenty-seven steps from the tailgate of His truck, carrying His toolbox.

Thud, thud, thud up the three wooden steps He built off the back stoop.

Stomp, stomp, one for each boot to knock the dirt off His soles.

Then He will bend over, undo the leather laces, loosening their grip on His ankles, then stand back up and use the toes of His left foot to push down the heel of the right boot.

He will do the same with the other boot.

His key slides into the lock, a low grind of metal before the Master lock turns to allow His entrance into the house.

The door opens and He enters, pushing it closed with a socked foot and setting His tool belt down. The hammer claw caught on the arm of the wooden bench and dangled there.

"Baby, you here?"

He is loud, but not yelling.

"Babe?"

He takes a step into the kitchen but does not see me, the marble-topped island between us.

"I'm here," I answer, without standing up.

He smiles, I bet, baring His teeth a little.

You aren't here, and there is no camera to show you, but if there was, you would see the sun streaming in through the panes of glass that He measured and fitted down both sides of the door. He stands between those rays, a silhouette, while I appear illuminated, the window light reflecting off the floor and into the wisps of my pale hair.

I'd spent the last hour bleaching and scrubbing, soaking the stain, hoping to lighten the dark place. I contemplated white paint, and, for only a moment, considered blaming Isaac.

Maybe this upsets you. You question what kind of mother I am.

You don't know what He is capable of. Maybe you think I am over-reacting, the way I thought my own mother did when she set a glass of water on the new dining room table one afternoon, later hiding the ring with a table runner, playing dumb when my father found it, acting like she had no idea how it got there, her face blanched with fear.

And really, up to this point, you would not have seen any signs that He hits me, or pinches that soft place at the back of my neck while we wave goodbye to my family at the front door. He has His arm around me. That is all you would see.

Perhaps He doesn't kick me moments after the door shuts, and tell me to get my fat ass upstairs and clean up the mess they left. They probably screwed in that bed, He screams. Your mother is a whore just like you, He might add, kicking me again. You wouldn't see the bruise, purple as this stain on the kitchen floor.

But if you were watching now, you would see me bracing for the pain, the memory of the last time still fresh and ripe as those berries. Or wrapping my arms around my body to protect the baby grow-ing inside me, a second baby that I do not even want, because if He finds out, He will want the baby, and I might remember how gentle He was while I carried Isaac, never once raising a fist or foot to me. And I might forget how He walked into the nursery, watched me lay newborn Isaac in his bed before shoving me down onto the floor and pushing right into me, while I tried not to scream or wake the baby. I might forget how He got up on his knees and buckled Himself back up, while I stayed curled up, knees to chest, gripping the wooden leg of the crib.

You didn't see any of this. You want to put these pages down, because you don't want to believe this was happening without anyone knowing. But you do believe me, and you are afraid. Compare your fear to mine. Resist the urge to turn away. Feel the fear of what is coming, and imagine that my fear must be ten times, maybe a hundred times bigger, because I will feel the pain while you walk away from this unharmed.

⚫

I would walk away too, if I could. I can only survive the next hour by slipping outside of myself and watching what happens as I am watching myself recorded on that camera. I pretend that I am as far away from all this as you are.

⚫

He walks back, entering the kitchen on sock feet.

He rounds the island, sees the pie on the counter, sticks His finger in, breaking the intricate lattice strips she has woven in and out across the top. He licks His finger.

He stops when He sees her kneeling on the floor, her back to Him.

He sees her arms moving back and forth, piston-like, working at something.

He comes closer, peers over her shoulder to see the purple lines, dark canals between the three tiles, which she has been able to reduce to a grayish tone.

Finger still in His mouth, He does not move.

His jaw muscles tighten. It appears He may bite off his own digit. Shit.

Goddamn it. You know that tile was special order, He screams in her ear, from a customer who changed her mind. He's not even sure He can get it anymore. She stays in her place, her eyes darting back and forth, deciding whether to move and make Him chase her or prostrate herself, let Him see her on her knees, working at the stain. She stays knelt on the hard floor, bends nearly into child's pose.

Please, let me explain, I've been trying to get it up all afternoon, after you said you hadn't sealed it, she says.

So this is My fault?

No, no, I didn't mean that. I'm trying to tell you how it happened is all.

You lied to me.

No. No.

When I called, you didn't say anything about this. If you had told Me then, I could have come right home. Now this has penetrated all the way through. There's nothing I can do to fix it. Nothing except start over, rip the whole damn thing up.

He reaches for her shirt and pulls her up to standing by the neck of it.

Then He shoves her back down.

Get out of My kitchen, He says, although He still has hold of her shirt.

He kicks her buttocks, so her lower half pushes forward while the fabric of her shirt pulls at her airway and His hand keeps her head close enough that His breathing rustles the hairs at the back of her neck.

He puts His left hand against the small of her back, so she cannot turn around, and pushes her forward. Her hip bone knocks into one corner of the granite countertop. At the doorway, He lets go of her neck and shoves her onto the hallway floor, where she spills into the pool of sunlight.

She stays there, for now. He turns back to His floor. He takes a steak knife from the drawer. My imaginary camera stays on her, but you can hear Him scraping the knife into the grout, gently, bit by bit, so He can lift the tile out of its place. Right now, He cares more about the tile than about punishing her. He will get to her later.

I hear Him muttering to Himself on the other side of the island. She—I—we pull ourselves upright. I have to do something to keep myself tied to my body. I don't want to disappear again.

I don't want to die. I don't want to leave my little boy.

I put my hand to my hand to my throat, breathe in and out. The skin hurts, but I am grateful for that. I want to feel this pain. It is mine, this pain, this body.

I won't let him do this to her anymore. I will not watch him hurt her again. I will wrap myself around her like a silken thread and lasso her to me.

•

I move toward the doorway, lean my arm on the wooden frame. My bare feet move across the tile until I am close enough to see his head on the other side. He is talking to himself, muttering words I cannot hear. Still, at the sound of his voice, I feel the thread spooling out, losing its tension. The steak knife is on the counter, beside my empty bottle of bleach. I make myself pick up the knife. I hold it in my hand; he stands up.

"I told you to stay out of my kitchen."

The sound of his voice threatens to unravel me. I have to stay right there, so I put my hand with the knife down and put it to the skin of my forearm, pulled it across. Blood wells up, a thin red line, rising until it overflows and runs down my arm and drips onto the counter.

"What the hell are you doing?"

He takes a step toward me. I can tell he is worried about what I will do.

I push the knife in again, deeper this time, and the blood runs faster, just enough to frighten him and remind him I am in control. I turn from the island, like a castaway on a flimsy raft, my arm reaching out to him. One fat drop slithers down my arm. It splatters onto his white tile.

He looks at it, at me, back at the floor. I have never seen him unsure of himself. His breathing quickens, almost a pant.

The sunlight has shifted now, revealing the wrinkles at the corners of his squinted eyes, darting between me and the floor.

•

I make one last cut, turning my hand over and running the knife across my palm. I straighten my arm, let my blood fall to the floor, squeezing my hand into a fist. Blood forces itself between my fingers, running to the tips, spilling onto his bleached tiles, one drop on top of another, so close together that the drops of blood merge and became larger. He does not move.

I stay there too, the thread that ties me to myself growing stronger, taut.

LININGS

Verna married

Vernon

Vauthier in October 1931 wearing a

mauve-colored wool coat. Underneath she wore one of her frayed dresses from St.

Vincent DePaul. She stood in the chapel, beneath a statue of the

Virgin. Sweat beaded and ran down her back, but she kept her coat on.

•

It was the only beautiful thing she owned.

•

May I take your coat for you?" asked the young nun standing beside her.

Sister Marie Celestine was not just a nun. She was gentle (the word soft comes to mind). She would be Verna's new sister-in-law, a gentle smiling woman. She was the one who had requested permission for the newlyweds to be married on the campus of this tiny college in rural Indiana. She was the only family Vernon had left. He wanted her present at the ceremony. Since she was not allowed to leave the campus, the two of them came to her.

•

At seventeen, Sr. Marie Celeste was young, even for a novice. The Sisters of Providence had made an exception because her older sister Margaret had come to the order thirteen years ago. With special permission Sr. Marie Celeste finished her high school education during her novitiate. This fall, she would begin her college studies. She planned to study music and perhaps attend the Cincinnati Conservatory. She played piano, and also violin, thanks to the patronage of the Sisters at Sacred Heart Elementary School, which all the Vauthier children had attended.

Years after she witnesses Verna and Vernon's wedding, Sr. Marie Celeste will return to Sacred Heart as a teacher, where she too will reach out to young girls who might be ignored if not for the eye of an attentive young nun. Most of the families have little money for books or music lessons. As a young girl, Marie read the books the nuns kept on a shelf beside the hymnals and the Bibles: *Jane Eyre, Little Women*, and others. And because only women were permitted to enter the private living quarters of the convent, no one realized the girls were being taught much more than cooking and embroidery.

•

Verna grew up on a farm in Posey County, the only girl in her family for three generations. No one had offered her books or music lessons. Her mother taught her to cook and to sew. She had gone to the small parish school, where she was taught by the priest, then went straight home to help with chores and take care of her younger brothers, hoping to find enough time before dark to complete her arithmetic problems and sentence diagrams.

Now she looks over at the only other woman in the room, who will soon be her sister by marriage.

•

As a boy, no one had taken notice of young Vernon as the nuns had of his sisters. He was just another son of another man whose entire life was spent working in the brewery and drinking at the bar down the street. The priesthood would not have been an option for him. At twelve, already Vernon had the worn, rough hands of a carpenter, marked with ink stains from his weekend job at the Courier, where he changed the big rolls of paper on the printing press before the Sunday edition.

•

The three of them stand like ambassadors from three foreign nations, as close to family as any of them have. They are like pieces of a dress loosely basted together but easily ripped apart.

•

"That is a beautiful coat," says Sister Marie Celeste.

"Thank you," Verna answers, blushing a lighter shade of the wool's deep color, and after a second or two adds, "I made it myself."

This impresses the novice. She too sews all her own clothing and that of many of the nuns. But nothing she has ever worn is this beautiful. The wide collar is embroidered with looping vines to resemble those of the melons that grew on Verna's family farm. A seamed bodice nips in at her tiny waist. (At five foot two, Verna weighs just shy of one hundred pounds. During her first pregnancy, she will gain only eleven pounds and will wear the coat home from the hospital, unbuttoned on a cold February morning, with her baby tucked inside.) Top-stitching on either side of the seams lends its wearer a sense of importance, like a gilt frame around the Mona Lisa.

Buttoned up to hide her faded dress, the coat holds its greatest treasure close to Verna's breast: a heavy satin lining cut from the remains of her mother's ivory wedding dress.

Sister Marie takes Verna's hand and smiles. She lifts that hand to the soft flesh of her own cheek, the patch of her left exposed by the stiff white headpiece. What do I say to a woman on her wedding day, Marie Celeste wonders. She has no wisdom to offer. She is a Bride of Christ.

Next year, Marie will wear a wedding gown when she takes her vows. She assumes hers will be one of the many kept by the order, those worn by the other sisters, gowns that are worn and then worn again by girls whose families do not have the means to buy one or borrow one from someone in the family. After many years of being worn, the gowns are dismantled, seams removed, and the fabric reworked into satin linings for the sisters' coffins. Marie, as a gifted seamstress, will do much of this work, as well as the more frequent tasks of cutting and sewing the long black habits of their daily wardrobe, until Vatican II loosens the rules governing their clothing.

•

Verna has a lifetime of beautiful clothes to sew.

And she will have many beautiful things—bright patterned full skirts and sleeveless blouses with darts to hug her bust line—but that will be years later, after she and Vernon divorce. For now, this coat is the only lovely thing she owns, and she will cry real tears when she must take it apart, ripping out the double row of seams so as not to damage the fabric. At first she will only remove the lining, which felt right coming as it had from her mother's dress. She will use the satin to make a baptismal gown for her tiny baby girl. The gown will gather at her fragile neck and fall past her scrunched-up feet. Its simple design will be untraditional; no lace or ribbons will edge its hem. The long sleeves will bell out at the ends, covering the blue tinge that will bloom beneath the baby's tiny fingernails. Verna will take one long strip and fashion something like a Japanese obi that wraps around the infant's middle and knots in the front. It will be beautiful, and everyone at church will tell her so.

The coat will still be beautiful without its lining, but years later, when Easter comes early in March, Verna will use the rose-colored wool to make a miniature version of the coat for her daughter. Katherine's heart will barely keep blood pumping through her body during warm summer. The little girl's lips will turn blue by the time they walk halfway to church every Sunday. They will need to leave an hour early for mass, stopping halfway there for a cup of tea at an elderly neighbor's house. Katherine's tea will be mostly warm milk, but the time it takes to heat up will give her heart a chance to recover.

But that Easter will turn out to be colder, with fat snow flurries flying in the background of the photos they take their Kodak camera, the blue-lipped girl in her rosy coat flanked by her mother and the aunt.

By that Easter, Sister Marie Celeste will have been called to Sacred Heart to teach. The principal, Sister Rosemary, a short, stocky woman with dark bangs shooting out from beneath her veil, will call Sr. Marie to provide music instruction at the school, where Katherine is in first grade.

•

As a teacher, Sr. Marie will hear stories from her young students, told in that matter-of-fact way of young children who do not know that these things should be kept private. She will hear about drunken fathers who return late after spending too much money at the tavern. She will hear stories from her sister-in-law too, who worries about being home alone with her sickly child. Sr. Marie will wish she could bring them home with her, to the Motherhouse in the summer months. There, one feels a camaraderie that she realizes most women will never know. Two months to pray and study and rest is not part of most women's lives then, or now, but it is a regular practice for the Sisters of Providence. Katherine, she thinks, would surely blossom in the company of so many women and not one man, save Christ.

At least Sr. Marie will be allowed to watch from the upstairs window as Katherine enters the school building each morning. The principal will not allow her to be the girl's teacher, but at least she will be close by, close enough to slip an extra milk carton onto her lunch tray if she times her daily stroll through the lunchroom properly.

From her classroom window, Sr. Marie will recognize the mauve color of the wool coat. Verna has kept the collar intact. It will look extravagant on the thin child, too fine for her faded jumper and scuffed shoes. The nun who teaches first grade will frown when she sees it, thinking the parents frivolously spent money on a fancy coat instead of new school uniforms. Only Marie will know what that coat cost her sister-in-law. She imagines Verna cutting into the heavy, rose-colored fabric and pain shoots through her own hands.

She will finger the rosary around her neck, the one that was her sister Margaret's, that should have been buried with her. She will remember how at the last moment, allowed to enter the chapel and say goodbye privately, the living sister switched rosaries with the dead one. It had not been easy; Margaret's hands were as stiff as her starched collar. She had tried not to think of this body that was no longer the older sister she had grown up with. Despite being surrounded by her Providence family, Sr. Marie Celeste felt entirely alone. She had been at the convent for only three short months when Margaret died.

When Marie sees the coat on the child, she will say a secret prayer for Verna, for strength. She never knew about the secret lining, because on the wedding day, Verna kept the coat buttoned up. Sr. Marie remembers how the other nuns pursed their lips, thought the new bride vain when at the evening service she resisted their offer to take the coat and hang it up for her.

Yet even without knowing about the lining, Marie feels that common thread that always tugs at her when she thinks of Verna, a different feeling than what she has with the other Sisters of Providence. She knows it is a sin, to feel this allegiance, and yet she makes no attempt to alter her heart. She continues to carry this allegiance with her after she is called back from Sacred Heart.

Years later, after their second daughter is born, twelve years younger than Katherine, Vernon writes to say he has left Verna and has remarried. Marie will not be permitted to attend this second wedding; her brother is now an adulterer in the eyes of God. Marie never meets their second daughter or his second wife. She writes to Verna, who in return sends photos of the girls, one in which the younger daughter wears a frayed but recognizable mauve-colored coat. Katherine, a teenager by then, blooms into embroidered bell-bottom jeans and a navy peacoat, a red turtleneck hiding the scar from her surgery.

•

Sr. Marie had been only nine years old and still known by her baptismal name, Ruth, when she watched her mother fold and lay the old wedding gown into the suitcase that her older sister Margaret was taking to the convent. A few months later, the family drove to Terre Haute for the ceremony where Margaret took her final vows. The young novices walked up the aisle of the great cathedral one by one, dressed in white gowns, some from their own mothers or aunts, some borrowed from the convent. As one, they knelt in front of the bishop.

Ruth had recognized her mother's dress on Margaret's blocky frame. It gaped at the chest and pulled at the shoulder seams. At nine, Sr. Marie could already see where it might have been altered to fit properly, but the women had sworn off all vanity. Later, after laying their bodies prostrate on the pink marble floor, the new sisters entered a tiny vestibule in the back, where their hair was sheared off and they removed the wedding gowns in exchange for their black habits and veils. Her mother's gown was taken away and stored with the other gowns. Marie did not think to be angry that her mother had given away the dress that she might have worn to her own wedding someday. She hoped she would wear that dress after all, when she took her own vows of celibacy and poverty.

•

Three months after the sisters were reunited at the Motherhouse, Margaret would be dead.

Sr. Marie pulled the dress out of storage, ripped out the seams holding it together, cut and reworked the fabric until only scraps remained, reshaping it into the lining of the casket.

•

Vernon had not been able to get off work for his sister's funeral. Even if he had, he didn't own a car and he didn't have money for the gasoline. He had made a toast to Margaret at the tavern that night.

"To my sister," he said, raising his glass. "Thank God one of us is a saint."

He meant it in a kind way. He was making fun of himself. He knew he would never be that good. He could only hope that someday, after he had passed on, his two sisters' good works would atone for his sins.

•

A few months after Margaret's death, Vernon called Marie to say he was getting married and asking if they could come to St. Mary's for the wedding. Margaret's death gave her the courage to ask this favor of the priest. Margaret would have wanted to keep their family stitched together. Maybe Verna was the thread that could repair them.

He'd stopped drinking, Vernon swore, because Verna did not like it. He was going to turn his life around.

They drove to Terre Haute the next weekend, Verna in her rose-colored coat with its satin lining. Sr. Marie Celeste, draped in her stolen rosary, met them at the heavy iron gates of campus. She wore her own secret finery, a scrap of her mother's satin tucked into the bodice of her undergarments.

•

No one had expected Sr. Marie to sew the lining for Margaret's coffin. In fact, the other nuns had been a little put off by Sr. Marie's insistence on making it herself. They saw this as a form of vanity, her possessiveness; Margaret had been their sister too. Though she was no longer a novice, they tried to be understanding. They let her take on the project, though they stayed close by, supervising her work, partly out of desire to be close to Margaret, and also to make sure the sewing was done well. When Sr. Marie joined the order, they had expected another sister like Margaret, a friend who would make them laugh and never let anything get her down. They couldn't have known how different the two women were, or that Margaret would spend so much time looking after her quiet, fragile younger sibling in her effort to rescue Marie from the future she would have had if she had stayed home to marry and have children, if she had stayed in the house with their father and brother.

On the dusty rack, Sr. Marie found the gown—the one their mother had folded into the green suitcase, the one that lay between Margaret and the pink marble floor when she took her vows. The one that would now be dismantled and resurrected as the lining for her sister's coffin.

Sr. Marie had seen dresses transformed for the older nuns who died, but this was different. Their vows certainly did not guarantee long life, but most of them did live into their eighties and nineties, as Sr. Marie Celeste would. She had been expecting to spend those years in the company of Margaret. She appreciated the other women letting her have these precious last hours, the only ones that would not feel lonely for a very long time, until the year she went to teach at the school where her sickly niece Katherine spent each day. And though Marie did not yet know that child, not while she was sewing the satin remnants into the box, she spent those long quiet hours remembering her own childhood, how Margaret had protected her from the neighborhood children, the taunting that ended with Margaret dragging an older boy off of her and pinning him to the sidewalk and punching him in the chest and stomach and throat until he gasped for breath. Or when Margaret had stepped between her brother and younger sister, putting herself in Marie's place while he grunted and pulled at Margaret's nightdress and then silently slumped on top of her, sometimes even falling asleep between them but always gone in the morning. Or Margaret washing out her nightgown by hand and hanging it up to dry before they left for school.

Marie had never discussed these secrets with her sister, uncertain if she was protecting herself or her sister from the shame. Maybe both of them. But she knew she had to sew the lining to repay that debt.

•

Her brother lives a long life. He had long since started drinking again, early in his marriage to Verna, who stayed until their daughters were grown. By then he is consuming two cases of beer a day. When he calls, weeping, Katherine says of course, she will come and get him. For the next two decades she buys his beer and cigarettes. She doesn't complain about the smoke-filled house when her cardiologists asked how things are at home.

She and her younger sister lose touch. Neither she nor her mother will visit since Vernon moved in.

At night, Vernon talks in his sleep, apologizing to his sisters, his wife, his daughters.

By the time of his death, the church has loosened its rules and he is given a proper funeral, presided over by the priest at Sacred Heart.

•

When her brother had called to tell her he was getting married, Marie thought he had changed, that marrying Verna would heal him. Sr. Marie Celeste was a Bride of Christ, as was Margaret, both pure now in His eyes, no matter who had touched them before. She thought, naively, marriage could work that same miracle with her brother.

The couple arrived in the morning, dew still on the grass. Sr. Marie Celeste walked them around campus, pointed out the grotto of Mary and the cathedral where she and Margaret had taken their vows. The pink marble, she told them, had been brought over from France. She walked them around the path to the cemetery, row upon row of white crosses inscribed with each sister's name and her years of birth and death. She took them to Margaret's grave, its new grass glowing with the green of spring.

From there, they walked under the cathedral of trees to the shell chapel. Sr. Marie Celeste swung open the gate, stepped inside. The walls were entirely covered with shells that had been imbedded in the plaster.

Sister Marie Celeste dipped her fingertips in the holy water. She touched the four signs of the cross to her forehead, her heart, her left and right shoulders. The shock of the cold water was like stepping one toe into the ocean. Vernon stepped in behind her and repeated the sign of the cross. Verna was the last to do so, after removing her gloves.

At the row of red votive candles, Sr. Marie pulled a thin wooden stick from a bowl of sand, touched it to one of the lit flames, and held it up to a fresh wick. It burst to life while she said a quick prayer for her dead sister. Vernon dug into his pocket. He pulled out a handful of coins and dropped them through the slot of a metal box. The sounds of the coins jangling as they hit the bottom echoed in the room.

Marie lit three more candles, one for each of them.

Shadows on the walls became their wedding guests.

"Father Raymond will be here soon," she told them. "He is coming straight from mass. It's All Saints Day."

They stood in silence, Verna and Vernon holding hands until they heard the priest's steps crunch up the gravel path. He entered through the opened gate and smiled at them. A large, white-haired man wearing the black cassock and collar of his vocation. He shook hands with Vernon and offered a slight bow to Verna. When he turned to Sr. Marie Celeste, she bowed her head and closed her eyes to receive the priest's blessing. With his thumb, he made the sign of the cross on her forehead.

Including the ghost of Margaret, the women outnumbered the men, as they usually did on this campus. Father Raymond took up the remainder of the space in the small chamber. They made an intimate party.

But for Marie, this event was more closure than beginning. She felt as if she was returning a favor to her sister. She couldn't explain why, but she felt herself a conduit for forgiveness, on behalf of Margaret, a letting go of the past.

Decades later, after Verna had left Vernon for another man, after Katherine had the surgery that repaired the hole in her heart, after Vernon had been taken in by his adult daughter, after Marie had earned her master's degree from the Cincinnati Conservatory of Music and taught in fourteen different parochial schools, the old nun languished in a nursing home, wondering who would sew the lining of her coffin. She still kept the scrap of yellowed satin tucked into the Bible beside her bed.

•

I came across the scrap of cloth when I visited the convent, twenty years after her death. The nun in charge of the archive room had laid out Sr. Marie Celeste's things on a large wooden table: photos of the two sisters taken with their mother, prayer cards, yellowed newspaper clippings, letters from students (one stack from a woman who sent a letter each Christmas, detailing her life as a wife and mother), her death certificate, her obituary, her diplomas and college transcripts. She was a straight A student all the way through graduate school.

Later that day, in the warm afternoon sun, I walked out to the grotto. Years of constant drip drip drip had darkened the stones. I walked past the shell chapel, which was kept locked to ward off vandals. I walked to the cemetery. I walked row after row of identical white crosses until I found them. Though they had died more than fifty years apart, the sisters were buried side by side. Somehow, by some miracle of God or women, the grave beside Margaret had been saved for Marie, safely laid to rest beside her sister.

I laid down on the grass between the two graves. In one hand, I held tight to that scrap of yellowed satin. In the other, a small piece of mauve-colored wool. Somehow, I felt, I must make of this a new garment.

DOORS: REVISED

EVERY NIGHT MY DAD WOULD FALL ASLEEP watching the ten o'clock news. Then he would rise from the couch and check to make sure the front door was locked before going to bed. I suppose he thought this kept us safe.

None of the doors inside the house locked, not even those leading to the bathroom. There were two, one from the living room and the other from my parents' bedroom.

Our bedroom had no door. The five of us slept in one room, boys on one side, girls on the other of a half wall down the middle, open at the top. My sister and I shared a bed under the windows on the girls' side. My grandmother's walnut wardrobe faced us from across the room. Its doors were missing as well.

Dad said the doors had been damaged in a fire. He wanted to repair them, he said, before he rehung them. Most projects in our house—a wood-burning stove without a chimney or flue pipe, purchased in the seventies when my dad decided we should heat our house the old-fashioned way; a six-foot-tall statue of St. Francis of Assisi covered with a quilted furniture pad and awaiting replacement fingers on his outstretched hands; a secretary desk that had belonged to my mother's grandfather, stored in the workshop for decades until my mother touched the thing and it collapsed into a pile of sawdust—remained incomplete, so our clothes hung exposed for most of my time in that house.

At some point, on a visit back home after I had graduated from college, gotten married, and given birth to the first of three children, I noticed the cabinet doors had been replaced. Black scars showed where the flames had marred the wood.

Strange that the fire missed the ornately carved drawers at the bottom, but my father remained tight-lipped about the details.

•

My father—Vince—was a boy when his mother died. He was not the youngest, so he was not pitied. He was not a girl who lost her confidante as she was about to give birth to her first child, like his only sister. He was not the man of the family, left alone to care for six children. Alone and overlooked, he was left holding a grief as dense as the coconut cake brought to their door by old Sister Matilda.[1]

This cake turned out to be the only comfort he could find in those first days after his mother's death. He hid it on the top shelf of the wardrobe, in the room he shared with his two younger brothers. Perhaps that memory is what led him to accept the apprenticeship with the baker, arranged when Vince's father realized that his son had still not returned to school two weeks after the funeral.

Elizabeth Schafer Brenner, Betty to her neighbors and family, entered the hospital on May 8, 1947, to undergo surgery for cancer of the stomach.[2] The doctor removed a tumor that grew so fat, Betty

---

1 She wasn't old then, but she was when I met her. We visited her at the convent every Christmas. She dug into a deep freezer in the kitchen and pulled out cellophane-wrapped coconut snowballs.

2 Vince was diagnosed with the same disease in December of 2004. In March 2005, he underwent surgery. Afterward the doctor told him that less than 5% of patients survive the surgery. Of those, only 20% live five years. Twelve years later, Vince is still cancer free.

had noticed the waistband of her good dress becoming snug. She was used to holding a bit of weight until her babies weaned[3], and with the Depression, and then the war, her babies fed from her breast for a good long time. Elizabeth had seen Vince turn away when the little ones crawled up into her lap.

She died from an infection at the incision site.

She lived long enough to hear the doctor say that the tumor was the size of an orange. She remembered those great bulbous fruits, purchased with her precious egg money and stuffed into the children's shoes on St. Nicholas Day. She remembered the children at the kitchen table, the spray of citrus oil filling her nose as they peeled the fruit. She died with the scent of oranges in her nostrils.

George[4] wanted to bring the children in to say goodbye, after the surgeon told him that Elizabeth was in God's hands. The hospital staff refused his request.[5] The last person to see her alive was not the priest, who had come to give her last rites, but Sister Matilda, who held Elizabeth's cold hand long after George could not.

Matilda, who brought the coconut cake, who saw the sadness in Vince's eyes, who later arranged to have the boy apprentice at her brother's bakery.

•

---

3 It was common for women to breastfeed their children for economic reasons, and to make up for food shortages during the Depression and the War. Vince says he remembers seeing mothers nurse their babies while riding the streetcar.

4 George Brenner was my grandfather. Vince told me that he died in January of 1967, one month after my birth, but when we went to the cemetery to visit their graves, I noticed that his death was actually in January of 1966, almost a year before I was born.

5 Children have not historically been allowed into hospitals, not to protect the children but to protect the patients from germs brought in by them. By the time Vince was diagnosed, these rules had changed. I would be able to breastfeed my five-month-old daughter in the waiting room and later at his bedside.

Matilda and Elizabeth met when they were girls.[6]

By the age of eighteen, both of them had committed to a life of service, Matilda, or Tillie to her friends, to the church, and Betty to her future husband and children. Both saw their choices as devoting their lives—body and mind—to God. They stayed close, Tillie living at the convent across from the church, and Betty around the corner on Columbia Street.

"God is in the pots and pans," Matilda said to her friend when they were working in the church kitchen one Sunday dinner. They had served nearly a thousand people that day, or at least it felt that way. The line wound out the door all afternoon.

"Right now, I wish God was in my feet," Elizabeth said, easing her bloated body into a chair.

Tillie set down her rag and knelt in front of her, taking Elizabeth's shoes, one at a time, and slipping[7] them from her feet.

"Are you a nun or my mother?"

"I'm a nun, Betty," Tillie answered, smiling at the joke. "And I'm devoted to a life of service. I'm also your friend."

"A friend who refuses to be this baby's godmother."

"We've been over this," Tillie said, kneading the balls of Betty's feet. "I would if I could. I'm not permitted to make that kind of vow to anyone but God."

"I've taken a vow too, to love my husband, but if I had to choose between you and George, I'm not sure the decision would so easy."

"Let's hope you never have to choose." Tillie looked up at her friend, whom she expected to see smiling. Instead, her eyebrows were

---

6 I made this up. I really do have an Aunt Matilda, my grandfather's sister. But Matilda and Elizabeth did not meet until they were grown women.

7 Tugging, more likely, as Betty's feet were probably quite bloated by this stage of her pregnancy, and they didn't have money to buy her another pair of shoes.

knitted together.

"Promise me this. Promise me you'll look out for him."

"Who? George?" Now she was definitely smiling.

"My son," Betty said, her voice dropping low and serious.

"What makes you so certain this is a boy? It could be another girl."

Elizabeth ran her hand around her belly in circles, her fingers bare of jewelry now, her wedding ring on a chain around her neck.

"I just know, that's all. Everything about this one is different than with Alice. Everything this baby tells me is that he is my son. Call it faith. Call it hope. But it is a boy. It has to be."

It was a boy, but not her only son, as she had hoped.

John came after Vince. Then Lawrence, Peter, and finally Francis, the baby. By then Elizabeth knew what she had been sensing was not Vince's boyness, but something beyond even that. He had never been of her but only came to the world through her. Her body carried that baby but never owned him. One might think this suggested a distance from her son, but in fact it was his separateness that opened the door for a closeness that she never had with her other children, even her only daughter. Vince never relied on her the way the others did. Rather he became a companion, a fellow traveler, growing up while she looked on. She never taught him to tie his shoes or write his name or butcher a chicken. He brought these accomplishments to her, after his first success.

But Vince also did not pitch in to help her, unless asked. He never volunteered to teach the young boys how to tie their shoes, or even bend down to tie their shoes for them. He wasn't mean or spiteful; he moved in his own world, and assumed everyone could take care of themselves.

•

The day of her funeral, he tied his only tie, a gift from his godparents, and slipped on a borrowed suit coat. Two weeks later, her dressed himself in the same clothes to meet the baker, and again, minus the suit coat, when he carried away his remaining belongings in the small leather suitcase his father had given him.

"It was your mother's. There's a hat box and a vanity case too, but I gave those to Alice. I didn't figure you have much need of them."

Vince took his mother's suitcase, rode the streetcar downtown to Fourth and Columbia, jumped off and walked two blocks east to the bakery, and finding the front doors locked, because it was Sunday, entered the bakery through the back door with its painted sign that read DELIVERIES ONLY.

His father would remarry six months later. He had to, he said later in confession.[8] He had not been touched that way for so long, and he needed someone to comfort him, to look after him. The younger boys, anxious as their father to have someone, let her put them to bed and read to them and tie their boots before sending them off to school.

His new wife would pack up Elizabeth's clothes and personal belongings and give them to the Little Sisters of the Poor. She would sell some of the furniture to an antique dealer for thirty dollars, to make room for her own things. But she would keep Elizabeth's old brass bed. She would ask George to plant it in the garden as a trellis for beans. Its rails would support a bumper crop that she canned and served all year. She was a good gardener. The one thing she failed to harvest were eggs in the winter months, as Elizabeth had.

Vince saw these things unfold in stages. Each time he came home, it was as if a page had turned in the story that used to be his own. He began to fear what would have changed by the weekend.

---

8 As confession is private, I could not know this. I do know, however, that my maternal grandfather married a woman after he had sex with her, because he felt obligated to by Catholic Law.

During the week, he kept his distance, except on Wednesdays when his father's new wife came into the bakery for bread. It was a perk of his apprenticeship. Vince brought fresh bread every Saturday when he came home to go to mass with the family and sleep in his old bedroom. By mid-week, though, the bread was eaten. She could have sent one of Vince's brothers—he would have been happy to see them—but she insisted on coming herself.

"Vincent, Frannie's taking his First Communion this Sunday at mass. I was hoping you could bring a cake for lunch after at our house."

Vince, who was decorating wedding cakes by then, knew that he was capable of doing a cake for the twenty or so people who would follow them home after mass. He remembered his own First Communion, how his mother sent him out to gather eggs. She needed a dozen for her angel food cake. He carried the wire basket full of eggs in shades of brown and taupe, some spotted with reddish freckles like the ones on his mother's arms. He watched as she separated the whites from the yolks, cracking the shell and pulling the halves apart, tipping the yolk from side to side, the whites sliding out and running into the blue bowl on the table. The yolks, plopped into a smaller bowl and put in the icebox, would be used to brush the tops of rolls before they were placed in the oven. Some might be fed back to the chickens, mixed in with their mash and scraps. Nothing in his mother's kitchen went to waste.

Vince had started keeping a few chickens of his own in the little yard behind the bakery. The baker was happy to be getting eggs for free, especially as the weather turned cold.

"Not sure how you do it, Vinnie. I haven't had to buy eggs all winter."

"I told you I could keep those chickens laying, Mr. Hermann."[9]

9 My dad says that his mother added crushed hot peppers to her chicken feed in the winter, which caused them to drink more water. He said they don't drink enough water when it's cold, and water is what is

"Yes, you did, Vinnie," he said, winking at his wife who was rolling out dough for cinnamon buns. "You've been a godsend."

·

Vince arrived home on Saturday carrying the baker's cardboard box. He had baked a white cake and decorated it with meringue frosting. Vince used his new set of decorating tips, purchased by Mr. Hermann with the money he said he'd saved on eggs.[10] He used a large star tip to create a border around the top and bottom edges. Another tip, with a slit that curved and widened at the base, formed white roses; these had been made a day ahead and left to set up on butcher paper overnight. A third tip, notched with a V, made leaves. Vince began close to the base of each rose, pulling outward, and with a twist of his wrist formed the frosting into tapered fronds with ruffled edges. Finally, with a fine-pointed tip, he wrote Frannie's name and the word "Blessings" in light blue script. The fluffy white frosting and flowers made him think of his mother's feather bed.

He handed the box to Francis with a serious look on his face. He was pretty sure Frannie did not remember their mother's angel food cake. He hoped not. Vince didn't want his little brother to feel he was missing anything today. Of all the younger brothers, Vince most wanted to please Francis. But then, everyone wanted to please Francis. His smile was the closest things they had to Elizabeth.

Frannie did smile, broadly, then turned and showed the cake to his stepmother.

---

essential to laying eggs. Now that I keep my own hens, I have read that chickens cannot sense heat in spicy food. Rather, the decreased sunlight of winter days causes the reduction in egg production.

10 My dad still has these decorating tips. The clear plastic top is cracked and gummy to the touch. He stored them on a shelf in his basement and made wedding cakes for each of his children with them. This year, he gave all of them to my thirteen-year-old daughter.

"Look, Mommy, Vincent brought me a present, just like you said he would."

"It's a good thing too," she said, peering up at Vince. "Here it is nearly the end of March. You'd think I would be getting at least a dozen eggs. I never get extra to sell. If they don't start laying soon, I might have to sell more of the furniture."

By this time, the brass bed wore two summer's worth of tarnish, so green it looked like it had sprouted out of the ground. The chickens roosted on it, especially the gentle Barred Rocks, which had been Elizabeth's favorite.[11]

Vince looked around at the new furnishings. An overstuffed sofa covered in heavy floral fabric and two chairs faced the corner fireplace. A large oak table surrounded by slatted chairs occupied the kitchen.

The only room that had stayed the same was the one that Vince shared with Francis on his weekend visits. Two narrow beds sat below the windows, and the old wardrobe that had been his mother's faced them from the opposite wall. One of its doors closed with the twist of a wooden block inside; the other always stood ajar. The brass key had been lost long before Vincent was born.

Even though he would only stay one night, Vince unpacked his clothes and hung them inside the wardrobe's vast belly. He hung up his suit jackets and looped his only tie over the neck of the hanger. Closing the doors, he pressed both hands against the smooth dark walnut, then slid them down along the grain, as if he were stroking a great dark horse that needed to be settled. When he removed his hand, the one door creaked open just an inch. He rested his left ear on the wood. He waited to hear his mother's voice the way one listens for waves in a seashell.

---

11 This is why I named my first Barred Rock hen Betty. She was so gentle she would walk up to me and let me hold her in both hands, cupped together, and sing her to sleep.

The wardrobe stayed silent.

"Vincent? You in there?"

He heard her footsteps on the stairs and quickly slid his suitcase under the bed.

"Oh, here you are," his stepmother said, poking her head through the doorway. "Your father's home. Dinner is on the table."

She stepped all the way inside and held a hand out to him.

"I can't thank you enough for Frannie's cake. He is so excited."

Vincent smiled.

"I know it is not what your mother would have done."

She waited for a response from the dark, curly-headed young man. Perhaps if Vince had been living at home still when his father remarried, he would have felt differently about her, saw how much she did for his brothers: mending ripped jeans, bandaging scraped knees and elbows, rubbing their father's shoulders when he came home grouchy. All Vince knew was her beggar's face at the bakery every Wednesday and her hands harvesting beans off his dead mother's brass bed.

Vince said nothing.

"I was cleaning out the wardrobe this week, and I found the strangest thing. A cake plate. Can you imagine? It still had crumbs on it."

"Why were you cleaning out the wardrobe?"

"Frannie doesn't need this old thing. It's empty most of the time. I've been thinking of moving his bed in with the other two boys. Did you know he has nightmares? I thought if he wasn't sleeping alone, he might be more comfortable."

She paused.

"Soon you will stop coming home to stay."

"Why would I do that?"

"Vincent, you're young. You can't be an apprentice to Tillie's brother forever. She kept you from the draft before, but that can't last. Besides, the service might be good for you, especially now that you have a skill. The army needs bakers too." His stepmother looked sad. "Most of your friends have signed up by now."

"Mr. Hermann is her brother?" Vince asked, even as he was figuring it out. He knew Mr. Hermann and Sister Matilda were related, not because he ever saw them together, but because he saw her picture on the kitchen wall. The sister wore her white habit with its wide wings on either side of her head, the two of them standing under a tree, walnuts littering the ground and the church's tall steeple in the background. He remembered the black walnut fudge she sent to his mother every Christmas. He'd heard from his mother how she and the nun had been close friends. He was smart, even if he had dropped out of school, and he could put two and two together. And he also knew, although he had not thought of it before, that a high school dropout was eligible for the draft.

"You don't know anything about anything," Vince said, looking at her with such fire in his eyes that she stepped back as if to keep from being burned.

His stepmother stood still, a safe distance from him, then turned to walk downstairs. Vince heard her heels clicking on the wood, the creak when she turned on the landing. The clicking faded as she reached the first floor and called everyone to the table.

Vince sat down the bed, the mattress sinking beneath his adult weight. His stomach growled for the food whose scents filled the house like smoke before flames: roasted chicken, fat dumplings in broth, green beans canned with bits of bacon, and in their cut-glass dish, dark pickled beets with purpled onions from the bottom of the jar. Seeing the empty place at the table, his father would wait a moment then look around to find his wife's face, perhaps see the sad look in her eye. After that, he would go ahead and say grace.

"Bless us, Oh Lord, and these thy gifts which we are about to receive from thy bounty, through Christ our Lord. Amen."

The words reached up to Vince, called him to the table.

He could have gone. He could have chosen to stand up and walk downstairs to his place at the table.

But all those years of grief, beginning with the hidden coconut cake and the brass the bed bearing the weight of beans and Barred Rocks, this small bed on which he crouched, rubbed against him like flint, a wall of heat that kept him from rising up and being received into the open arms of his family.

And rather than let himself go and let himself love her, or at least accept what she had to offer, he pulled the lighter from his pocket, flipped back the lid, placed his thumb on the strike, and pushed the flint until a flame burst up.

Vince held it up to the curtain fluttering at the drafty window of the old house.

And when the breeze reached in and extinguished the flame, he did it again, this time catching the curtain. He sat there watching the fire rush up the windowsill faster than any person could run.

The smell of smoke overtook the good smells of dinner below him.

The feet of his father thundered up the stairs.

Vince saw the flames licking at the ceiling, the sparks flying across the room, catching the rug. He saw the frightened faces of his brothers in the doorway before his stepmother gathered her arms around them and pulled them to her and hurried them down the stairs and out the front door. When Vince turned to the window, they were in the front yard looking up at him. Through the glass, he saw their faces, frightened of losing another person they loved, and still, Vince sat on the bed, unwilling to help his father, who was hauling buckets of water and throwing them onto the rug, yanking down the curtain and stamping out the sparks. His father raced back and forth, just a blur in the smoke. Vince watched the first flames lick at the doors of the wardrobe. The heat rushed over him and it felt good to have this balance, finally, the heat inside his body with the heat out here in the world, where someone else could quench it.

His father pushed open the window and threw the sopping, smoldering rug out onto the ground. Vince heard the sizzle as it the cold, wet dirt.

•

That day defined my father for the rest of his life. He had already drawn himself as someone who lost everything when he lost his mother. But on that day, his father and stepmother and brothers realized they had lost him as well. With surprisingly few angry words, my grandfather forgave him, but Vince never spent another night in the house, choosing to spend his weekends at the bakery, in his little back room, studying for the high school equivalency exams.

He signed on with the Marines. Sandwiched between World War II and the Korean War, he spent four years baking bread and biscuits and cakes for the soldiers.

After that, he met my mother, married and bought a house. Then a bigger house, with enough land to put in a garden and keep chickens, where I shared a bed with my sister in the back room. The wardrobe, with its missing doors, stood guard over us, our clothes exposed to everyone who entered.

A few years ago, they decided to renovate that back bedroom. My dad asked if I wanted to have the wardrobe.[12]

When the movers delivered the wardrobe, I assembled it according to my dad's instructions. Its design was like a puzzle. Staring at

---

12 In their will, my parents have listed special items that they would like each of their children to have. I have always been meant to inherit the wardrobe, so when they no longer had a use for it, they decided to give it to me ahead of time. My older brother was supposed to get my grandfather's secretary desk. Unfortunately, while cleaning out the house, we found the secretary in pieces, consumed by termites.

the pile of labeled slats and wood pieces, I could not imagine it as the massive piece from my childhood. The sides and back pieces fit into slots at the bottom. Two wooden drawers with carved, curved handles notched into place. It took two of us to lift the top and set it down, stabilizing the outside walls.

In the bottom of the crate, the doors lay wrapped in gray furniture quilts. My husband and I lifted first one and then the other from their protective nest and laid them out side by side on the living room rug. The wood gleamed, freshly oiled.

One door was perfect, the grain's pattern like ripples in a pond.

The other bore the scars of my father's anger, its center panel cracked and bubbled. The veneer was blackened with the shadowy shape of a face, like the portrait on an old cameo. And though my grandmother had died twenty-five years before I was born, she rose up before me, a phoenix from the ashes, her arms reaching for me. She smelled of cake and woodsmoke. Her touch was feather light on my cheek. For those few moments, I too was unblemished and new.

FERTILE

THE HOUSE ON THE PIE-SHAPED PLOT of land is the only family home Trey remembers. When he was a boy, he visited his grandparents here, spent the night in the small bedroom upstairs when his parents went out of town. When he was twelve, his parents bought the house for $1. That bedroom became his own.

Now it is Trey's house.

When his mother died, his dad retired and bought a small condo in a subdivision where the old Catholic girls' school use to stand. His dad fishes and takes naps and studies Spanish for thirty minutes every day. He has a martini at five o'clock. When he goes to a neighbor's house for dinner, he makes his martini in a Ball jar, screws a lid on top, and takes it with him, just like his wife used to do for him. Heath Jr. sold the house to Trey, for considerably more than one dollar but still a fair price, the economy being what it was. Heath Jr. said he didn't need that much house anymore. Still, he wanted it to stay in the family.

•

Trey, or Heath Leslie Brown III, is the first and only son to Heath Leslie Brown, Jr. and his wife in the first year of their marriage, followed a few years later by the birth of a daughter.

After high school, Trey attends the college that his father and grandfather and every male in his family have attended since his great-great-great grandfather served on the board of trustees at its founding 1855. After being rejected from medical school, Trey substitute teaches for a year and applies to graduate school. He is accepted at the University of Colorado to pursue his doctorate in biochemistry. He drives his parents' old Chevy station wagon cross country with a mattress tied to the top and his new skis, a graduation present from his grandmother, resting across the back seat.

In Colorado, he meets a girl from his hometown. They marry. She quits college in her final semester, seven months pregnant with their first child, a daughter. Four years later, during his postdoc in Michigan, they have another daughter, and finally, a son.

At his wife's urging, they move back home, where they buy a three-bedroom bungalow. He gets a job in a medical lab and teaches Intro to Biology twice a week at his alma mater. On weekends, he works around the house and plays with the kids to give his wife a break.

•

Now Trey is an attorney, like his father and his grandfather and his great-grandfather and his great-great grandfather.

Becoming a lawyer was never part of his plan.

•

He still remembers the day he had received a call from the chair of the Biology Department at his alma mater offering him a tenure tract position. He hung up the receiver of the phone mounted on the wall of the lab and went out to find a payphone so he could call his wife. He didn't want his dick of a boss to overhear. Trey would need to keep this job until the end of summer, when his teaching contract would begin.

In the lobby, he dropped a quarter in the top slot, heard it clank through the phone's innards, then dialed his home number. Martha picked up on the first ring, probably on their new cordless phone sitting beside the bed, where she lay with the baby stretched out the length of her torso.

He had wanted to celebrate, maybe take the family to dinner at the Iron Skillet.

He had been teaching one biology class each semester, an evening class, mostly to adults, initially for the money. At the time, being handed a check for $1,800 seemed huge; that was before he calculated the hourly breakdown based on how much time he put in. Trey invited students home for study groups and lab help, his daughters playing restaurant in the breakfast nook while he sat at the dining room table, keeping an ear out for the baby while the white plastic baby monitor crackled on the counter, his wife out with friends, having given Trey the tag-you're-it sign on her way out the door. He couldn't blame her. She was home all day with all three kids while he was at work and in class.

She was a good mom. She just needed a break.

But now he had been offered a full professorship at his alma mater, the same college as his father and grandfather. His grandfather had been a national champion diver. His father, a Hall of Fame football player.

I will be a great teacher, he thought.

•

Trey did not accept the job. They did not celebrate with dinner at the Iron Skillet.

When he heard Martha's voice say hello on the other end of the line, he told her his news.

Martha feigned excitement, hung up, and called her family. Her brothers made some calls and got the law school to accept a late application on Trey's behalf.

•

Martha and her brothers had convinced him that he could not support a family on a professor's salary. Trey could not bring himself to call the department head and turn them down. Instead, he stopped answering their calls, let the answering machine pick up, then erased the messages. Instead of researching the best biology textbook for his students, Trey stopped in the financial aid office to sign promissory notes for $50,000. He registered for night classes, which he would attend after long days in the lab, still working for his dick of a boss. He donated bone marrow to make a couple hundred extra bucks when they needed the cash. He graduated in three years when Nate, their youngest, was four.

•

Nate was five when Martha said she wanted a divorce.

She wasn't happy, she said, on their way home from a party, a wedding reception for one of his law school buddies.

He chalked her comment up to being drunk, but the next morning, she said, I meant what I said last night.

Trey moved into a flimsy, three-bedroom ranch one neighborhood away from their house, so he could be close to the kids.

He wished he could stop answering her calls.

He wished he could stop pulling into the driveway of the house, standing in the entryway on cherry floors he had laid, while Martha called the kids in from the trails he'd blazed in the three-acre lot behind their house.

He wished he could stop picturing the bedrooms that held his children every night while he laid down his head in crappy prefab on a concrete slab.

The only thing going well was his work. In his firm, he was known as the settlement king, mostly scientific inventions and intellectual property. Even though it wasn't flashy trial cases, he brought in billions of dollars, thanks to three days a week and every other weekend without the kids.

•

When Trey's father suffered a heart attack, then needed knee surgery (the cost of being a Hall of Fame football player), then buried his wife, Trey agreed to purchase the home that had been in their family for three generations.

His father said, "I need someplace with no stairs, but I can't let it go."

He said, "We lived in that house together for thirty-eight years."

He said, "I wish I could afford to give it to you or your sister the way my dad gave it to me."

Trey understood. He'd lost his home; he had to keep his father from losing his too.

•

His sisters pledged to help with family gatherings, which he would now host each Christmas, and to help decorate the kids' rooms. His dad left most of the furniture that had come with the house when he bought it from the Hibben sisters.

Every other weekend and two nights a week, Trey's children stayed at the house with him, gathered around the same table where his mother had served dinner. They did homework while he cooked. They played the Manners game, a stack of quarters in front of each place, which they handed over to Trey if they forgot to use their napkin or chew with their mouths closed. Then the kids excused themselves and went to their rooms, where they plugged into their laptops and iPhones, like every modern teenager, and the house grew quiet.

But as quiet as that was, it was nothing compared to the quiet on nights when they were with their mother. Those nights, he worked late. He played golf or rehearsed with the church choir, arriving home after dark to eat a dinner of graham crackers and milk straight from the jug. He went up alone to the bedroom that had once belonged to his parents. Back then he had to knock before entering. Now he hardly ever closed the door. There was no reason to.

He could live without sex, he thought. He could live on solitary dinners of graham crackers and milk. He could clean his own toilets and take the kids on vacation by himself. The one thing he still could not do was fall asleep alone in the big house.

He had let go—of the dream of tasting his grandfather's omelets, of the hope of going to medical school, of the idea of teaching, of his marriage and the home he had cultivated into something meant to last forever.

He found himself, at fifty, alone in the house of his childhood.

He could not go on living this way: barren.

•

In early May, wearing boxers and a white undershirt, Trey slipped his feet into his old Timberland hiking boots, the ones he'd had since his Colorado days. He meant only to step out onto the patio for a few minutes to breathe in the cool night air, to clear his head, but the moonlight reflected off the yellow dandelions in such a way that he reached down, nestled his fingers close to the roots, and wiggled and eased one out of the ground. It was the most satisfying feeling he could remember having in a long, long time. He reached for another. This one came up more easily, grounded in the sandy soil at the edge of the brick patio. He wiped his hand on his shirt and left a smear of dirt.

He continued to move along the edge, laying each ruined weed side by side, a mass grave of dandelions. If anyone—his kids or a wife—had been there to see him, pulling weeds in his underwear by moonlight, they would have knocked on the glass and beckoned him inside, motioning that he was crazy. But no one was there; he was free to kneel in the damp grass, moving brick by brick until he looked back and saw the straight, cleared line of his progress along the length of the patio to the fence line.

The sky was beginning to lighten. Exhausted, he stumbled inside and fell asleep in the lower bunk of his sons' room.

The next morning, he woke with dirt caked beneath his fingernails and ground into the skin of his knees, his boots still on.

He showered, dressed for work, and drank a cup of coffee standing at the kitchen counter. He backed his black Suburban out of the driveway, looking into the rear window, maneuvering around the stone pillars that stood guard at the end of the driveway, keeping his eyes averted from the front lawn. If what had happened last night was a dream, he didn't want to know yet. But the when he pulled in that evening, the wilting pile of weeds was waiting for him at the edge of the patio.

That night, he turned his efforts to the raised bed was full of redbud and maple starts. It had rained that evening; he quickly cleared the large bed without the use of a trowel and hauled the new pile across the street to the creek bed.

On the third night, Trey raked and cleared and leveled the dirt in the bed.

On the fourth night, he stopped at the nursery on his way home from work to buy topsoil. At the corner, he pulled into the drivethrough tobacco shop for a pack of Marlboros. He changed his clothes and headed out to the yard, hauling plastic bags of dirt out one by one and lining them beside the empty bed where his grandmother once grew azaleas.

Trey squatted on the ground and took the cigarettes from the pocket of his shorts. He pulled one out with his lips and lit it. An orange glow blazed against the skin of his cupped hand. He inhaled deeply then let out the trail of smoke, dropped the lighter and Marlboros back into his pocket and turned to the bags of soil, ripping each one open and dumping them until he had one great dark mound of damp dirt.

With the cigarette gripped between his lips, he dug both hands into the pile and pushed it outward in all directions, smoothing it by running his hands back and forth. Though it was dark, he could faintly see the difference in color between the new dark dirt, more like coffee grounds or the color of his once-dark hair, the old soil faded and gray with age. When he finished, he stepped back to survey his work.

He had done a good job. It looked soft and smooth enough to lie down in.

•

The went untended for the next few days. The kids were there and needed his attention. He was not ready to explain the stained T-shirts and dirty fingernails. He didn't want his smooth soil transformed into miniature battlefields or scooped into pie pans to become the crust for rose petal tarts and leafy quiches. The bed belonged only to him.

It was just after dawn on Sunday morning when he returned to the small plot. The air was cool, the grass wet on his bare feet. He stood beside the dark rectangle and lit a cigarette, saying a silent thanks than none of his children were up yet.

An animal had dug several holes in one corner, some kind of search and rescue mission. Trey wondered if the creature found what it was looking for.

What's next, Trey asked himself, taking a long drag and blowing out the smoke before he flicked the bit of ash to the ground.

The kids returned, and he sat down to help his oldest daughter Amber with a history report. She wanted to plant a garden like the Native women did, with corns and beans and squash that grew up together in the same soil.

"They lean on each other, Daddy, like sisters. That's why they call them that. The Three Sisters," Amber said, sitting at the table making a diorama in a shoebox while he cooked dinner: two boxes of Kraft Macaroni and Cheese, little smoked sausages that the kids drenched in Log Cabin syrup, and creamed corn. He set the ranch dressing and ketchup out too.

"We should plant a garden like that, Daddy," Amber said, looking up from transforming a Polly Pocket doll into a Miami woman with fabric scraps.

"That sounds great," he told her, stirring the soft noodles into the orange powder and melted butter. "But you can't just plant a garden. It takes time, and a lot of work."

"We could do it together."

He could still see her head of red curls pulled into a lumpy ponytail (unlike the tight French braids his ex-wife could do), stray strands sticking out while she bent over her project.

He called the other kids in to dinner while Amber carefully moved her project aside. The kids tumbled into their seats, talking all at once. Nate farted. The others laughed.

That night, as he sat in the dark smoking, he remembered the glass case of arrowheads and relics his grandfather used to keep in the living room, each item labeled with where it had been found.

Most of them came from a grassy area behind the old house with a circle of twisty trees. Everyone said it was a Native burial ground. Trey remembered it as a weedy patch behind the gas station where he went to buy his grandfather pipe tobacco sometimes.

He remembered something Amber had said at the table, that

the Delaware Indians had farmed this land for centuries before white men settled it.

•

By June, the corn was halfway up his calf. He had followed the diagram he found online: measuring five feet between the mounds; digging four holes, six inches apart, on each mound; filling each hole with corn kernels; then the beans at each corner, creating an imaginary square like a constellation around the mound. Staggered between the corn-bean mounds, Trey planted mounds of squash. He chose small sugar-pie pumpkins, thinking that the kids could use them at Halloween, should any of the vines actually produce fruit. He had considered zucchini or yellow squash, but he wasn't sure he would know what to do with them. He didn't want his harvest to rot on the ground.

Six weeks later, tiny vines were beginning to trail across the ground, with magical tendrils that he wrapped around his finger the way he used to do with the curls on Amber's head. He wished he could time-lapse the growth of the vines, so he could watch them twist and turn and grasp onto twigs and stems, reaching and reaching for something.

By the Fourth of July, his corn was, as the saying goes, knee-high.

He decided to stay home for the holiday. The kids were at their mother's annual family barbeque. His father and sister were down at the lake.

His sister had called him every day the week before, trying to convince him to come along, finally stopping by unannounced one evening, which was how she became the first person to find him working in his little garden. She got a little teary.

"So far the soil has stayed pretty moist," he said. "Honestly, I hadn't thought about whether or not I should be giving them additional water. I'm just going on instinct."

"Well, let me know if you need any help." She started to get back in her car, seeming for a moment to have forgotten why she stopped by. "You sure you don't want to come to the lake?"

"I'm sure."

"You're welcome to ride down with us, you know."

He knew she'd say that. "I know. I'm just not sure I want to be there by myself."

"You wouldn't be by yourself. The whole family will be there."

He could see she regretted saying this right away. It was not something she had to think about, trading the holidays, batting kids back and forth like shuttlecocks. Winning and losing them and winning them back, but only momentarily. It would happen to her too, he knew, when her kids grew up and had their own lives and invitations from friends and in-laws. But right now, that was far off for her.

"Have any other plans?"

"Nope. Just working around here," he said, pushing a bunch of pulled weeds into a pile.

"At least let me drop off some food on our way out of town. I'm making potato salad and a breakfast casserole for the next morning."

"Sure, that sounds great."

She slid into her car and shut the door. She rolled down the window and leaned her arm over the edge.

"Hey, as long as you're going to be here, would you mind checking on my garden? It may need a little water, and there will probably be more tomatoes ready to be picked if you're interested."

"Sure, I can do that."

She rolled the window up and backed out of the old iron gate.

Already the weekend did not sound as unpleasant as he had expected it to. He would have potato salad and maybe a few fresh tomatoes from his sister's garden. He could sit and eat on his patio, drink a cold beer, maybe grill a steak.

Turning back to his garden, he counted the enormous yellow blossoms on the pumpkin vines, traced the first, tiny, needle-like beans. The corn was taller than he initially thought. He didn't see any sign of fruit, but the stalks were strong as wood stakes. He could feel the rest of it waiting there, just out of reach.

A friend emailed me yesterday. She wrote, liberty is a funny word, isn't it?

I looked it up.

It means *the state of being free within society from oppressive restrictions imposed by authority on one's way of life, behavior, or political view, or the power or scope to act as one pleases.*

LIBERTY

LORETTA LOVED FULL SKIRTS and high heels and strands of cheap costume pearls.

She loved her two girls, Agnes and Alice, and being able to provide for them.

She did not want anyone to know how she liked to stand in the bathroom, before stepping into the tub, to admire the new muscles in her arms and calves, now etched with the sharp, straight lines of a pencil drawing, how instead of making her feel masculine, her new body made her more maternal. She was taking care of her girls, protecting them.

While she went to work, her girls were home with Loretta's mother-in-law. They helped weed and keep up the garden. They tended rabbits to supplement the family's meat rations. Loretta's mother-in-law took pride in making sure they had enough, trading any abundance for other needs.

Mr. Schuler the druggist would haggle with the old woman. Like everyone in the neighborhood, he knew it was not unusual to find at least one double yolk in a dozen of her eggs. And she got eggs all winter long, when everyone else's chickens stopped laying altogether.

Only her oldest granddaughter knew the secret, because she was the one who mixed the hot peppers into the birds' mash every morn-

ing, to make them drink more water. Alice had not even told her
own mother.

This morning, when Loretta walked off the line, she found a
Ball jar sitting outside her locker in the lunchroom. It looked like it
contained pure white sand from a beach, or what Loretta imagined
sand would look like. She had never been to the ocean. She had read
about beaches and sandy footprints at the lacy edge of the tide, and
she believed that her knowledge from stories was enough for her to
understand and know these things.

Loretta sat down to take off her boots.

The jar held grains of sugar. She could picture the women she
worked with handing the jar down the line, each adding a couple of
tablespoons from home until the sugar piled up and slid down the
sides, piling up like the sand that came downriver on barges.

The women had done this so Alice would have a cake for her
sixteenth birthday. Loretta couldn't wait to get home and show her.

When she turned up the sidewalk of their block, she heard the
girls' voices in the backyard. What Loretta envied most about the
daughters was something she could never imitate: that they had each
other, someone to lie next to at night and tickle each other's backs
or wake up after a nightmare. She thought when she got married she
would finally have that, but it was not the same as what her girls had,
unconditional. When Loretta woke up in the middle of the night
and rolled into Leo, he would stir, then his hand would go to her
breast, cupping it, his lips searching for hers. His hips would push
into her, wanting, not offering.

Loretta stood at the gate, unseen, watching the girls and the old
woman at work.

"Look at this one, Granny," Alice called, her voice still girlish.
She was naïve for a girl of sixteen, maybe because so many of the
boys were gone.

"Set it in the basket," Agnes said, her hands on her hips, bossing her older sister. "It will bruise if you hold onto it like that."

They moved up and down the rows. The part of the yard that was not garden held the chicken coop and rabbit hutches, one for the males and one for the females. A brown-handled basket sat on the ground, mounded with produce: red and yellow tomatoes, green squash, crooked orange carrots with bushy tops that would go to the animals, and burly onions, shining white as electric bulbs beneath the clumps of dirt that clung to them.

The old woman was collecting eggs in a large blue bowl that rested in the crook of her right arm. Occasionally she reached into her apron pocket to toss corn to the chickens who ran about her feet, pecking at their own reflections in her sturdy black shoes.

Hideous, those shoes, thought Loretta. She had grown so tired of seeing her mother-in-law shine her shoes each night, the smell of the polish, the soft circular rubbing of flannel on leather. Loretta imagined those shoes must have made deal with the devil, because the older woman had been wearing the day they met, along with the one good dress she still wore. She would likely be wearing them when Agnes and Alice were middle-aged women. Nuns habits would change more in those years, with shorter skirts and visible tufts of hair across their foreheads and soft cardigans over white blouses. Laura Striker's dress and shoes would stay the same.

Agnes looked up from the garden and saw Loretta watching them from outside the fence.

"Oh Mother, guess what? One of the hens is brooding. Granny says it is a good omen, so late in summer."

"Really?" Loretta answered, in the mock questioning voice of a mother.

"Yes, and she says if we get chicks that Alice gets to name them, for her birthday."

"I have a birthday present too," Loretta said, smiling and waggling the jar of sugar. "All the girls at work chipped in. It's enough for a cake. That is, if your grandmother can spare the eggs."

Loretta, Alice, and Agnes all turned to the old woman holding a dark red hen, stroking its back feathers. The bird's eyes were peacefully closed. Laura was not smiling, but they knew she wouldn't say no, not to Alice, though they also knew that she disapproved. They'd heard her stories of growing up in Tennessee, how at hog butchering time, her daddy would blow up the pig's bladder and tie off the end so the children could bat it back and forth like a balloon, and how grateful they were for that pleasure.

"We didn't have jacks and jump ropes like you girls do. We had to make do."

Her mother-in-law was a good woman. She would never let any harm come to the girls. But Loretta resented her quiet way of being in the world, how she didn't care a hoot for clothes and shoes and pretty things. She was happy with her garden and her chickens and her ugly polished shoes that she got resoled each year, paying the cobbler with double-yolked eggs.

Knowing this, Loretta somehow felt duller in her presence.

"Well, we better get this gardening done," the older woman said, setting down the chicken to count eggs. "I guess we have a cake to bake."

While the girls and their grandmother finished up outside, Loretta went on in. The screen door banged shut behind her. She intended to head upstairs and take a bath before Leo got home. She would put on clean clothes, maybe even a dress and a little makeup, for Alice's birthday dinner. Before that, while the water ran, she intended to sit on the side of the tub and read Ruth's letter.

Ruth, the youngest of her sister-in-laws, who now went by Sister Marie Celestine, had been sent to London to work in a hospital. She wasn't a nurse, but she knew how to lay a washcloth on a soldier's forehead and read letters from home, or help them craft return letters that tried to sound hopeful. Perhaps most importantly, she worked for free. The war was taking its toll. There weren't as many women who could leave home. Ruth didn't have any family, or at least no one at home that needed looking after since Loretta and Leo moved in with her mother.

Loretta and Ruth had been friends since childhood, long before Loretta met and fell in love with Leo. Loretta had been saving this letter. She opened the paper, thin as onion skin, and read the words Ruth had written.

Dear Loretta,

I miss you and the girls. I am not certain if my work here makes a bit of difference. The doctors sew them up, but it is almost worse after that, these threadbare men, as if people can be mended as easily as a pair of socks. The sadness stays inside, a wound that does not heal, a festering abscess. Whatever they see when they close their eyes makes them try hard to stay awake. The ones who can see, their eyes are as dull as the boots we remove from their feet when they come in.

Loretta stopped reading, glanced at her own callused feet.

When she was a child, Loretta's father had taken her to the circus up north, in Peru. They sat in the front row. She ate popcorn and sipped lemonade through a paper straw. Horses galloped around the ring with beautiful women standing on their backs. A clown had dumped a pail of confetti on her father. She was shocked when her father laughed and brushed the bits of colored paper off of his head.

Afterward, he'd taken her backstage to meet the clown, who her father had fought with in the first war, the one before she was born.

Loretta hid behind her father as they entered the tent. Bob-O the Clown waved at her father to sit beside him. As they chatted, Bob-O pulled out a pack of cigarettes and offered one to her father, who took it, flipping open his lighter to ignite first the clown's and then his own. Loretta watched as Bob-O drew in smoke through his painted lips and exhaled, leaning back and sighing. Then he placed the cigarette back in his mouth and held it there, bending over to untie his shoes.

When he slipped the shoe from his foot, Loretta sucked in her breath. She was shocked; Bob-O's feet were the same shape as her own and her father's, instead of the wide flat foot suggested by the shape of his funny red oxfords.

She was at an age when the world was still as it appeared to be, no tricks. She would remember that day, all her life, as the day she realized people looked different than their clothes and makeup suggested.

When I get a day off, which they require us to do at least once a month, I try to get out and see London a little. It is not at all how we used to imagine it. Once I took the train out to Kew Gardens. There is no staff left to tend to anything but vegetables. The roses have grown wild, the poppies bloom in beds full of weeds. I walked through all the paths, touching trees and sitting in the grass. I found a little place in town to have tea, a place called Maids of Honor. The walls were covered in flowered wallpaper, and the old brown teapot felt so warm in my cupped hands. They had only canned milk, no clotted cream, but the woman served me a slice of a lovely, airy cake. Then she brought a small pot of jam (sometimes wearing this habit has its benefits) made from raspberries she had picked last July. She told me the tearoom began as a place for working women to take afternoon tea, women who had chosen work instead of marriage and family. They would come here for company at little tables for two or three, so they didn't have to be alone.

Loretta heard the thudding steps of her husband on the stairs and in the hall. She turned off the tub faucets. The footsteps paused. He knocked on the door.

"Loretta? I'm home," he said, his voice flat after a day on his feet.

She hesitated, not wanting to answer.

"I'm taking a bath."

The footsteps continued down the hall. That was how things had been since they moved into his mother's house, his mother who had moved her own bed into the front parlor and given her bedroom to the girls. She and Leo slept in a makeshift bedroom on the wide landing, which was just as well, since she wouldn't be able to keep working if she got pregnant.

Slipping into the tub, she listened to the kitchen sounds below, carried up through the open windows. She heard talking but couldn't make out words. She heard the lifting and closing of the lid to the flour bin, the open and close of the icebox. She pictured them lining cake pans and taking turns stirring the batter. She felt guilty sitting in the bath, leaving her daughter to bake her own birthday cake. The sugar was my gift, she thought, and anyway, my daughter is a better baker than I am.

I've been reading Shakespeare, at night while the patients sleep. I would have enjoyed seeing his plays on the stage. Did you know that in the original productions, men acted every role, even the female characters? In one of the plays I read, a daughter kills her father, and another one is about a man trying to change his wild wife into an obedient one, and there is one where a woman disguises herself as a man, who is, of course, being acted by a man anyway.

Loretta stopped reading. She rose up, water running down over her ropy muscles. When she reached for Leo's old flannel robe, she saw her bicep turn and flex. When she began working, the constant lifting and moving, turning and tightening of screws, left her feeling fatigued. As time went by, less time than she imagined, muscles revealed themselves. And as she rotated through the line at the factory, different jobs lit up new parts of her body. The muscles would burn and then build until she felt a strength she had not known before. It scared her at first. Now she knew she would miss it and did not know how she could go back to the way things used to be.

She stepped out of the tub and slipped her arms inside the sleeves of the robe. She folded first one side then the other across her torso and pulled the belt tight at her waist. The top bloused away from her body, leaving a gap in the fabric, and her breasts swayed, suspended in air, when she leaned down to pull the plug from the drain. She needed to hurry, to get dressed and get downstairs and attempt to help set the table, but she wanted to finish Ruth's letter. She sat down on the curled lip of the tub and turned the paper over to read the last of it.

On Alice's birthday, I intend to walk to Southwark Cathedral to light a candle for her. I discovered Southwark by accident. Even though it's not Roman Catholic, I feel more at home here than in Westminster or St. Paul's. The sister who greeted me on my first visit said Anglo-Catholics do everything that we do, except they don't follow the Pope. We pray for him, she said, but we don't worship him. I remember her words exactly.

It is peaceful there. Wrought-iron chandeliers filled with candles hang from the ceiling. On one side is a statue of William Shakespeare, reclining on a sofa (the church was his home parish), and on the other side is a statue called the Stone Corpse. It is carved with a sunken face and exposed ribs. I suppose most people would find it hideous, or frightening, and I might have too, before being here. Now all I see when I look at it are the women being sent to us from the camps. They have shaved heads and skeleton hands poking out of dark coats and gray dresses, gray from dirt and wear over months, maybe years. When the first trucks arrived, Loretta, I thought they were men, and I thought, Good Lord, how long since these soldiers have eaten? Their eyes were gaunt, their breasts deflated, their hips narrowed. It was only after one of them spoke to me that I saw what she was.

Loretta knew Ruth would have cared for each of those women as if she were her own daughter, with a sense of sadness, an impulse to let a cry escape but the discipline to hold it back so as not to startle this lamb who had been so cruelly sheared of her humanity. She knew that at first Ruth would be afraid to touch her, for fear that her touch would cause pain, practically nothing left but her spirit, which might be frightened away. Then a maternal instinct would rise to the surface, like when they were young and found wild baby bunnies, so thin-skinned they could see their hearts beating in their chests.

She pictured Ruth seeing to each woman with unflinching tenderness, how she must go home each night exhausted and spent after spoon-feeding them broth, warming their blankets on radiators, sneaking an extra pat of butter onto their dinner trays, sliding soft wool socks onto their feet, where even their toes had lost their soft pads of fat.

She heard each one cry out in her sleep, the names of children and husbands and sisters, and she knew Ruth wondered how many were lost, ten, hundreds, perhaps even thousands, for every one she nurtured. She knew Ruth must wonder daily if her endeavors would help them heal, help free them from ghosts, or if they would be forever tied to those they had left behind, and how on those days, it would be all Ruth could do to sit in a chair beside their beds, thinking that, like the baby bunnies, they needed first to know that she could be trusted. She imagined one of those women, weeks later, allowing Ruth to place a cool washcloth on her forehead without tensing every muscle.

Loretta would never have known how to approach them. She had always been tough where Ruth was soft, all callused hands and bruised shins and sunburned cheeks. Even in their girlhood, she wanted to be more feminine than she was but could not manage it. She'd always had an edge to her, the way her body did now.

Loretta folded the letter and pushed it deep into her pocket. She opened the door and padded across to the girls' room. She sat down at the vanity Leo bought for her after they were married, pulled open the bottom drawer and took out a small box of makeup. When she opened it, the smell of treasured powder rose up. There would be no more of these things until the war ended.

Using a small square of flannel, she applied pale powder under her eyes, across her forehead, along the jawline to her chin.

Then eye shadow, pink to bring out her eyes and make them shine.

The liner was cakey. She spat on the brush and swirled it around in the center until the black clump softened into a paste. She leaned in close to the mirror and rimmed her eyes with a thin dark line. Her eyes opened up, like shutters after a storm. Her blue irises bloomed inside.

A dab of rouge, rubbed in gentle circles.

Finally, she reached down and pulled out her red lipstick. She never wore it at home, but today, her daughter one year closer to being a woman, she would make an exception.

She dropped her chin and touched her lipstick to the right corner of her lower lip, slid it to the left corner and back again. Then shifting to the center of her top lip, she pulled down to one side, then back to center and down the other, like stroking a sleek mustache. She pursed her lips together, placed the scrap of flannel between them and pursed, leaving her kiss behind.

Her naked face had become a garden of desert flowers, the kind that wait ten, twenty years for a good rain before they bloom.

In the kitchen, Agnes was setting the table. Alice was laying placing fresh-picked blackberries in a circle around the top of the cake. Laura was stirring a pot on the stove. Soon Leo would join them.

Barefoot and dressed only in her husband's old robe, Loretta took the narrow steps down to the party.

ON THE BANKS OF FALL CREEK

It is late August. I am driving down a country road to locate the site of the Fall Creek Massacre.

I should be keeping my eye on the road, but I glance, when I can, at the carpet of corn on either side of me. It looks solid, thick, like the rug on which I would sprawl as a child to watch television on Saturday nights after mass.

If only I could lie down on these silky brown tassels, and they could hold me up, comfort me.

But this corn cannot hold me up.

•

I first heard of the Fall Creek Massacre in a play written for Indiana's Bicentennial celebration. The story is told from the perspective of one of the Native women who was murdered. Kneeling on the stage floor, she tells the audience, *No one knows my name.*

We will never know the names of the three women massacred by white men on the bank of Fall Creek. We do not know the names of their two sons and two daughters.

We know the names of the murderers, white settlers who urged two Seneca men—a third man was off checking his animal traps, and upon his return, witnessing the murder of the women and children, he ran away and was never seen again—into the woods under the guise of needing help hunting for horses. The white men shot them in the back. The murdered Seneca men were known around the area as Logan and Ludlow, the third as Mingo. No one knows if these were their real names.

•

As I drive into town, I see a banner strung across State Street proclaiming PENDLETON HERITAGE DAYS.

History and progress. There's no need to choose one over the other— you can have them both. Here in Pendleton, Indiana, we're living proof of that. –Pendleton Town Website

•

I followed my GPS, a woman's voice instructing me to turn right at Falls Creek Park.

There is a playground, the kind I remember from my elementary school: a tall metal slide, squeaky swings, a hive-like jungle gym. Pregnant moms sit on benches watching toddlers play, their older children back in the classroom. I follow a curvy road to the Pendleton History Museum. I park and walk up a pathway of engraved bricks honoring Pendleton residents.

IN MEMORY OF DON AND MARGIE PAUSEL
IN MEMORY OF ALVIN AND HELEN BROWN
IN MEMORY OF BILL AND FRANCE SHUCK
IN MEMORY OF SIDENY STONER
IN MEMORY OF IRA RUBY M WEATHERFORD
IN MEMORY OF THURL L. SMITH

A sign on the door announces the Heritage Days Quilt Show. I ask the woman at the front door if the museum has any information about the massacre.

Normally yes, she says, laying a knotty, manicured hand on her lips, but not today. I peer inside and see that the interior is draped with pieced quilts.

•

We do not know the names of the three women massacred when white men returned to their camp and shot them and their two sons and two daughters. We do not know the children's names.

•

I pay my $5 cash to get into the quilt show.

Names are everywhere.

On tags marking each quilt's maker and the name of the quilt.

On the sign announcing the famous quilting teacher and writer being hosted for the event.

I move in and out and around the quilts, pushing them aside to see the historical relics they are hiding.

A camouflage jacket with a patch embroidered with the name PALMER

A photo of Edward Vernon's ninety-eighth birthday party

A white bowl and pitcher loaned by Elbert Pike

Blue willow dishes owned by Dan Collingwood

A dress uniform jacket bearing the name MCCORKLE

A poster listing a reward for information about a fugitive named WILLIAM GOODWIN

A lace tablecloth donated by Elizabeth Wood

A cape worn by Dorothy Dillenbeck Jarrett as a nurse in WWII

I come to a glass case with memorabilia from the indigenous people who populated this land before the US Government granted land rights to white settlers in the Treaty of St. Mary two hundred years ago.

I have seen this treaty, touched the yellowed paper, run my finger beneath the signatures of Jonathon Jennings, Lewis Cass, and

Benjamin Parke on behalf of the United States and the X's of the Miami chiefs next to the English attempts at their names. At the Indiana State Library, a quiet-voiced librarian named Bethany rolled the treaty out on a cart. She lifted the manila folder, the size of a school posterboard, and opened it to reveal two large sheets of lined paper detailing the exact area being sold to the US in exchange for a small reserve in the north, later taken away when Andrew Jackson ordered Native people be marched farther west.

Arranged on the dusty museum shelves are: an Indian doll donated by Ruth Dickinson,

a 1930s popular print titled "End of the Trail," donated by Bob and Nancy Wynant, moccasins donated by Ruth Dickinson, 13 Indiana artifacts (including 4 axe heads, 3 corn grinders, 2 tomahawks, 1 hammer) donated by Jessie Foust.

I push a hanging quilt aside to reveal a calligraphy print of a Cherokee blessing.

May the warm winds
Of heaven
Blow softly on this house
And
May the Great Spirit
Bless all who enter here

Below is the only mention I am able to find about the massacre, a framed map titled

HISTORICAL MAP OF 1824 INDIAN MASSACRE
ADAMS TOWNSHIP MADISON CO INDIANA

In the gift shop, another glass case displays a coloring book about Pocahontas and a replica of a girl's calico sunbonnet, both for sale.

•

We don't know the names of the three women massacred by white men at Fall Creek. We do not know the names of their two sons and two daughters.

•

I ask the woman running the quilt show if she knows where I can find the memorial marking the Fall Creek Massacre. She thinks for a moment and then points me in the direction, saying I will surely have to drive there as it is too far to walk. Before I leave, I vote for my favorite quilt, Roundhouse.

•

Outside, I walk down the bank to the falls, fifty feet from the museum. I walk across the bridge to a tree under which rests a stone engraved with these words:

THREE WHITE
MEN WERE HUNG
HERE IN 1925
FOR KILLING INDIANS

•

I walk up a hill, another fifty feet, to the road. Here is the memorial marker with historical information about the massacre. The sign was installed in 2017.

I walk back down the hill and sit by the falls. Thunder rumbles in the distance. Clouds are rolling in. Hard drops pock the water's surface.

•

We don't know the names of the three women massacred at Fall Creek along with their two sons and two daughters. We do not know their children's names.

•

We know the women and their children and the men were members of the Seneca tribe. The Seneca people came here believing the area around the falls offered sanctuary in violent storms. The Miami Indians shared these hunting grounds with other nations. But the white settlers didn't share land; they owned land. After the 1818 Treaty of St. Mary's, the land belonged only to the farmers and white people. White men, tired of the Natives hunting on their land, tricked Ludlow and Logan into following them. They shot Ludlow and Logan in the back. The white men returned to the creek and murdered the three women and their four children. We don't know the names of the three women or their four children.

•

I stand at the edge of the creek.

A woman stands in the water. She has dark hair, loose, long, heavy, wet, hanging down her back. She is bathing in the creek. She has stripped off her dress and is scrubbing her skin with a softened piece of deerskin. It is August but the water is cool and goose bumps rise on her arms. Her two children splash close by in the shallow area above the rock slabs that form the falls.

Hello, I say.

She looks up from her bathing. She doesn't express any self-consciousness at her nakedness.

Hi, I say again, adding a small wave.

She holds up her hand, acknowledging but not returning my wave.

We both turn, as mothers do, at the sound of her children laughing.

She looks back to me.

Are you one of the women who was murdered? I ask.

She nods.

Can you tell me your name?

She shakes her head.

Why not?

She stares at me.

I can't make up a name for you in my story. It doesn't feel right. It would be a lie, just to make a good ending.

She tilts her head to one side, the water running out of her hair in a continuous stream to the water's surface.

I will tell them I have seen you.

She nods.

I will try to make them see you too.

She nods again. A smile returns, close-lipped, chin trembling.

I hear the children splashing again and look their way. When I look back, she is gone.

On the rock in the middle of the creek, where I had seen two turtles from the museum's side, I see now that there are three turtles. There were three the whole time, but the third one was hidden from view by the others. This turtle sits on a ledge, sunning herself, with her neck outstretched.

•

I exit the park along a paved path. A weeping willow bears a sign pronouncing the tree was planted in memory of Patrick Adcock. Small white plaques hang from chains on the branches of younger trees that line either side of the path.

IN MEMORY OF NELDA MCKINNEY
IN MEMORY OF VICKI JONES
IN MEMORY OF HAROLD MURPHY
IN MEMORY OF MAXINE MICHEAL
IN MEMORY OF VINSON HEPFER

IN MEMORY OF CARROLL JONES
IN MEMORY OF JOE GOODSON

•

We do not know the names of the three Seneca women murdered on the banks of Fall Creek in 1825. We do not know the names of their two sons and two daughters.

THE DISHWASHERS

My mom used to say to me, you remind me so much of my sister Ann. She did not mean this as a compliment. She meant, you make me feel the way my sister makes me feel.

•

Most holiday gatherings were at Aunt Ann's house, because it was bigger than ours, with a rec room in the basement and an extra fridge in the garage stocked with cans of Pabst Blue Ribbon and bottles of Double Cola and Ski.

At home we were only allowed one glass of Coke, half the bottle, on Saturday nights after mass, but at Aunt Ann's, we could grab a soda without asking, pop off the lid with the opener Uncle Darryl mounted on the wall next to his workbench. We'd put the thick glass rim of the bottle straight to our lips and feel the soda fizz and burn in the back of our throats.

After dinner, I would sit on at the bar stools along the kitchen bar and watch Aunt Ann do the dishes. She didn't bother with an apron like my mom did, just wiped her wet hands on her pants.

Aunt Ann pulled her new dishwasher out of the closet. The harvest gold appliance had a wooden top, made to look like a butcher block. But its smooth flat top was not worn, the way my dad said his mom's old chopping block was, so old that it had dipped in the middle from years of use.

Ann reached around to the back of the machine and pulled out two hoses. She hooked one to the kitchen faucet and shoved a second hose down into the sink drain with the garbage disposal. Then she pulled a handle and opened its square front door. She loaded the dishes one by one, the plates evenly spaced and nestled, the coffee cups and glasses in neat rows on the top rack. She poured powdered soap with blue crystals into a compartment on the inside of the door and snapped its lid closed. When the door clicked shut, the machine whirred to life with the push of a button. I heard the water spraying inside of the compartment.

"You should get a dishwasher, Carolyn. It's made my life so much easier."

"I don't need a dishwasher," my mother said, leaning against the countertop and pretending to look out the window at my cousins playing baseball in the back field. "I gave birth to five of them."

From my perch on the stool, I watched my mom staring out the window, her chin in her hand. The kitchen window at the house where I grew up looks onto a country road, cars rushing by on their way to the new subdivisions sprouting up in what used to be farmers' fields. Every night after dinner, two of us kids stood at the sink under the window. One washed; the other dried.

My dad moved us to that house to get out of the city. Our half-acre lot was meant to be his homestead. He planted a large garden and composted our food scraps and converted the shed to a chicken house.

He taught us to pick blackberries from the thickets that grew over an old wooden fence, weed the vegetable garden and gather eggs. We wore straw hats that he bought for us. We canned green beans and tomatoes and apple butter and pickled beets.

As a kid, the worst part of this was the way it tethered us to home, like our dog Tippy tied to a tree out back. All summer we worked, rising at seven to don our wide-brimmed hats, weeding the rows of vegetables and gathering eggs.

My parents wanted us to believe that this was the kind of work worth doing by hand.

•

Aunt Ann worked as a nurse.

The money from her job was good. She used it to buy new appliances, an extra TV for her and Darryl's bedroom where he went to watch games after dinner, and nice clothes for the kids.

I don't think she worked just for the money. She loved the work too. The day-to-day things like carrying lunch trays and fluffing pillows. She could see the way a patient who had been stuck in bed would relax as she scrubbed their back and arms with a soapy washcloth. She was good at inserting catheters. These tasks brought relief to people.

After work, Aunt Ann sat in the bleachers at her boys' baseball games, drinking Double Cola and yelling for the boys to catch the ball or get a hit. She doled out quarters to her youngest child, her only daughter, for bubblegum from the concession stand.

On the way home from the game, she stopped to buy buckets of KFC with mashed potatoes and biscuits. She dished the food onto plates that she later scraped and loaded into the lower rack of her new Whirlpool dishwashing machine. Out the window, she studied the stakes marking where men in backhoes would begin to dig the hole for the new pool the next morning.

•

My mom wanted us to believe that we lived without modern conveniences by choice. But the truth was we lived this way because we didn't have any money. We didn't have the money to buy a new dishwasher. Sometimes we didn't even have enough money to buy gas for the car. We drank powdered milk mixed with water in last week's jugs. We grew vegetables and raised chickens to save money, not to appreciate the value of homegrown food.

We spent summers canning the things we grew until the basement shelves were stocked and the deep freezer was full, while my cousins played ball and rode bikes through the neighborhood.

•

On a summer morning, Ann woke her oldest son and said he was in charge before she headed out to the hospital. Their dad had already left for the station, wearing his stained work shirt with GLASER'S TEXACO embroidered over the right breast pocket. After work, Ann knew he would stop at the tavern to have beers with Terry and Old Joe, his two mechanics, before heading home to eat dinner in front of the TV.

Ann rolled down the windows of her wood-paneled station wagon, a car my mom and dad would buy from her in a few years when she and her husband purchased a newer model. She lit a cigarette and listened to the radio. She sang along to Anne Murray. Her white nurse's cap sat on the seat next to her. When she pulled into the staff parking lot, she put the car in park to finishing smoking. Then she stubbed it out in the ashtray and tilted the rearview mirror toward her face. She pinned her cap into her short brown hair and checked her lipstick.

Ann had put herself through nursing school, with some help from her father and her sister. She had not wanted to take their money, but she knew she had to get out somehow. While Ann sat in her car getting ready for a shift, her children were staring out the family room window at men shoveling dirt to make a hole that would become their new swimming pool. By the end of summer, the water would be reflecting sunlight into her eyes. She would have to put her hand to her forehead to shield them when the kids yelled, "Mom, look what I can do" and jumped in.

Inside the hospital, Ann's rubber-soled shoes squeaked with every step she took toward the elevator. She was grateful when she was inside and standing still and letting the elevator do the work of carrying her up four floors. The doors opened onto the maternity ward, where she was picking up an extra shift.

This floor was noisier than other places in the hospital, filled with the sounds of crying babies, husbands and wives talking and laughing, the women in clean gowns applying pink lipstick and blue eye shadow.

Ann preferred to be in the delivery rooms, where the hard work, the grunting and sweating and pushing took place, especially now that fathers were allowed in the room, now that women were demanding to be awake and unmedicated during labor, now that more women were feeding babies from the breast instead of the bottle. New mothers were no longer silenced by gas masks to dull the pain of contractions and doctors did not finish the job by pulling a baby from its mother's womb. These mothers sweated and grunted through their labor.

•

When I was hospitalized at seven months pregnant, it was my aunt who sat beside the bed and told me that I was going to have my baby early. She was in town to inspect the local hospital for its certification as part of her new job for the State Board of Health. She sat with me because my own mother was afraid to drive three hours on the highway.

I had wanted to have a natural childbirth with no drugs or interference. She told me I was going to be induced with Pitocin and likely would have an epidural or a C-section.

After clocking in, Ann picked up the chart that hung outside her first patient's room. She read over symptoms, saw the stats indicating elevated blood pressure, noted the constant headaches, the visual disturbances. She walked into the room, where a young woman with a head of curly hair sat in bed alone, looking out the window.

"Good morning, Mrs. Morris. How are you feeling today?" Ann said. She walked to the side of the bed, set down the chart, and picked up the woman's wrist to check her pulse.

"Same as yesterday."

Ann smiled at her.

Mrs. Morris—call me Jennifer, she'd said—looked younger than twenty-eight, the age written on her chart. She had come in sometime during the night.

Ann patted her arm before placing the pressure cuff around it.

"Did your husband bring you in?" Ann had seen the ring on a chain around her neck.

Jennifer shook her head.

"My husband is out of town on business, in Japan. I told him not to go, but he wanted to get this deal tied up before the baby came."

"What about your parents? Can I call someone for you?"

"No. I called my parents, but they don't like to travel. I told them not to worry."

Ann looked at this girl, for that was how she already thought of her, perhaps because she looked so small in the bed, despite her swollen face and body.

"Are you sure you don't want them to come?"

"No, thank you. My husband will be home by the end of the week. And hopefully, I'll be home by then."

Ann sat on the bed. The plastic mattress crinkled beneath the sheets.

"Jennifer, I don't think you will be going home that soon. I suspect you'll have this baby by the end of the week."

"But the doctor said he was just keeping me for observation. He didn't even officially admit me yet."

Ann smoothed her skirt. She knew the doctor would never give a young mother the full story. She knew she could get in trouble for saying anything.

"You will probably will be here until the birth of your baby and that won't be too much longer, I would say by the end of the week, if that long." Ann knew how this would go. She had seen it before. The doctor had probably said that they wanted to keep an eye on her, see if rest brought her blood pressure down. But even if it did, all that meant was that she couldn't get out of bed until this baby was born.

"But the baby's not due for another six weeks." Jennifer looked at her, the way all new mothers did as they realized the vision they'd returned to like a rosary all these months was not how their prayers would end.

Ann inched closer to Jennifer's body, so their hips were touching, with only the thin sheet between them. "I think it's more likely that it will happen before then."

"No. No, that's too soon."

Ann looked down at the hand she was holding, plump with fluid. Her body wanted this baby out; it had recognized the invader as a threat.

"The doctor will give you some medicine to help the baby's lungs grow faster and then he will give you some medicine to start labor."

"What do you mean?" Jennifer said, her voice small. "No one told me that."

"I know," Ann said, patting the hand again. She didn't let go.

On her lunch break, Ann called home to check on the kids. Keith told her that the pool guy said they should be finished by Labor Day, in time for the cookout with her sister's family. Then she called the gas station to check in with Darryl, but he was out.

"He went to get some parts a little while ago," Old Joe told her, and she heard him take a long pull off his cigarette and exhale it before continuing. "Should I give him a message?"

No, she told him, she'd see him when she got home from work.

On Jennifer's chart, she saw the order for two steroid shots, one before lunch and the other after Ann had gone home. She made her other rounds, filling water glasses, remaking beds, holding the hand of a middle-aged woman pregnant with her fifth baby, a bit of a surprise the woman said, while the father paced. He was so anxious Ann sent him down to get coffee while his wife wept, hoping the tears would be over by the time he got back, and they were.

At the end of her shift, Ann stopped back in Jennifer's room. The young woman was sleeping. Ann didn't wake her. She sat down in the chair beside the bed to fill out charts she'd offered to help with at the shift change. When she finished, she laid her head back and closed her eyes. She wanted to go home, but it felt wrong to leave this girl alone. Ann had been in the hall when Jennifer called her parents, and she could tell from the girl's "I understand" and "I know" and "It's okay" that they were not coming. Someone should be here for her.

When the orderly delivered her dinner tray, Jennifer woke up and rubbed her eyes with the backs of her hands.

"Careful," Ann said, gently holding up the IV tube so that it didn't tangle.

Jennifer smiled. "What are you doing here?"

"I just needed a quiet place to sit and catch up on some work. I hope you don't mind."

"No. That's fine." She lifted the pink plastic plate cover and scrunched up her nose.

Ann laughed. "It will taste better hot. That's all I can say for it."

"Don't you need to get home?"

"My kids will be out playing until dark. They won't even notice if I'm not there."

"My parents said to call them if I need anything."

"If you were my daughter, I'd be here."

"You are here," Jennifer said.

"Just wait. You'll see. After this baby, you'll be offering to do anything to get out of the house for a few minutes."

Jennifer put a forkful of peas to her lips to keep from smiling.

•

A couple of hours later, when Ann walked in the door, the house was quiet. Darryl was not home yet. The kids had waved to her from their bikes as she drove to the end of the cul-de-sac. She set her purse on the bar and walked over to the sink. It was piled with bowls and cups. She turned on the faucet and let the water run until it got hot, testing it with the same two fingers she had used to check Jennifer's pulse. She placed the stopper in the drain and squeezed a dollop of pink dish soap into the sink.

Out the window, she saw the big hole that would be filled with clean water later in the summer.

By that time, Jennifer would have had her baby. Her husband would be back from Japan. Another baseball season would be over. She would invite her sister's family to a Labor Day cookout and remind them to bring their bathing suits.

But first, she would wash the dishes.

•

Twenty-five years after my own baby is born, I learn that my cousin's granddaughter has been life-lined to Riley hospital.

Karleigh was born at twenty-eight weeks, weighing one pound eight ounces. Her mother developed severe preeclampsia and had an emergency C-section. Karleigh weighs less than two pounds. She has been admitted to the same hospital where her great grandmother sat with me, ten minutes from where I live.

I offer to sit with her, so she won't be alone. Her own mother has to work and take care of her older daughter. My cousin Kelly texts me the room number at Riley and the passcode to get into the NICU.

I park in the visitors' garage and pass through the security entrance—opening my bag and walking through a metal detector—and take an elevator up to the NICU, where an attendant looks up my name. She lets me through the double doors, instructing me to wash hands at the sink station just inside.

I hang my bag and jacket on a hook to my right and push the soap dispenser, which squirts a pile of white foam into my palm. I wring my hands over and over, scrubbing between my fingers.

The smell hits me. It's the same soap from when my own preemie baby was here, the smell of my first weeks as a mother. I lift my hands to my nose and breathe in, the way some people do with a baby's head. I do this every time I visit.

I bring *Bats on the Beach* to read to her, and my own book, *A Field Guide to Getting Lost* by Rebecca Solnit, to read while she sleeps.

I enter Karleigh's room and see the little lump of her in the plastic isolette. Her hat has fallen off of her tiny head, exposing sprouts of dark hair. Her body is bundled in a mint-green bunting, a strip of white tape strapped between her nose and mouth to hold her breathing tube in place. I lean down and say, hi baby, I came to visit you.

The nurse greets me, reminds me to use the hand sanitizer by the door, and asks who I am. I am listed as Karleigh's aunt, even though I am her first cousin twice removed.

The nurse says, "After I do rounds, I'll pull up a rocker so you can sit with her."

The nurse changes her diaper, checks her vitals, and fills the syringe that, through gravity, drains milk through the NG tube into Karleigh's stomach.

The rounds take longer than expected. Karleigh's colostomy bag is leaking. They want to repair it without having to remove all the tape from her tender skin. They clean around the site, trading out the soiled mint-green bunting for a clean mint-green bunting. Then they turn her over, like a roast, and settle her in and push the dark blue vinyl rocker next to the plastic tub and leave the room.

I sit down. I open the porthole door and hold her hand. The rocker moves smoothly back and forth. It lulls me. I lean my head back. Karleigh's eyes open. She watches me.

I read *Bats on the Beach*, a picture book about baby bats who go to the beach at night and feast on moths and make toys of old straws and paper snack baskets and fly home before the sun comes up. Karleigh closes her eyes and by the time I finish, she is sleeping.

I lean back in the chair and read *A Field Guide to Getting Lost*, occasionally reading a paragraph out loud.

For the next several months, I visit Karleigh. I read *Make Way for Ducklings, Owl Babies, The Paperbag Princess, Where the Wild Things Are, Ferdinand the Bull, The Cookie Store Cat,* and *Blueberries for Sal*, all the old books I saved from when my kids were little.

•

One day when I arrive, the nurse asks if I would like to hold Karleigh. I sit in the recliner while the nurse and a respiratory therapist maneuver tubes over the sides and out of the open isolette and into my arms. They pin her tubes to my blue sweater. They warn me not to dislodge her breathing tube.

I feel the weight of her, not the five pounds of her body, but the responsibility entrusted to me by her mother who is home caring for Karleigh's older sister, who goes to work every day except Saturdays when she drives to Indy to visit, who pumps breastmilk all week to bring with her.

I feel the clicking of the respirator, in, then out, inflating Karleigh's taut lungs, stretching the tissue that shouldn't have to work this hard.

•

When the doctors say Karleigh can go home, her mom spends the night with me. I drive her to the hospital to learn how to change a trach tube. It has snowed ten inches overnight.

At the end of the day, I pick Kourtney up and we drive back to my house. While Kourtney fixes herself of plate of cooked carrots, noodles, and Swedish meatballs from IKEA, I get her a diet Coke from the basement fridge.

I set the cold glass bottle of Coke on the table, and that is when I see the connection. I see who I have become. I am the aunt, here when a mom cannot be.

The next day, I drive Kourtney back to the hospital for her twenty-four-hour solo shift taking care of Karleigh.

The day after that, I go to the hospital to say goodbye. Standing by the hospital crib, I feel, for the first time, like I don't belong there. Karleigh smiles whenever her mom speaks. I've just been holding space.

Kourtney does not fret over the wagonload of equipment going home with them or flinch when she has to wipe down the opening at the base of Karleigh's throat where the trach goes in.

I drive back home through the snow. There is a pile of dirty dishes waiting on me. This cold weather has frozen the water line going to my dishwasher, so I have to wash dishes by hand until the weather warms. This makes me smile.

•

Karleigh Thacker, fifteen months, of Evansville, Indiana, passed away at her home surrounded by her family.

FORGIVENESS

FATHER SHEPHERD PULLED ME ASIDE at my grandfather's funeral. He wrapped his arms around me so that my face pressed against the wool of his vestments. It was not a warm hug; it felt stiff and distant despite our proximity to each other. Shep, as everyone called him, nodded his head and smiled. His mouth looked wide and his teeth too big. He said, "I wasn't sure you would come."

"It's my grandfather's funeral. You thought I wouldn't show up?"

"When have you done what everyone told you to do?" He squeezed my shoulders and said, "He talked about you, you know."

I stepped backward, out of his embrace, and smiled. I had watched him during mass, wondering what I owed to this priest who still thought of me as an insensitive and rebellious child, though I am forty years old and have not seen him since I was half that. Now I looked at his face up close, it made a stark contrast to the Polaroid image in my parents' photo album—a picture of him with a wild-haired little girl, a photograph taken the Christmas that my sister and my parents went away.

That year, Fr. Shep said mass in our living room. We passed a pewter plate with OUR DAILY BREAD stamped into the metal. We tore chunks of bread right from the loaf, its chewy texture so unlike the foam wafers in church that melted and stuck to the roof of my mouth.

In the photograph I am wearing a long red velvet dress with an eyelet pinafore on the front. He is bouncing me on one knee, and I am laughing, with my head thrown back. I can nearly hear my laughter, little girl giggles that made my belly hurt. My mother had gotten the camera as an early Christmas gift that year; my dress had been another. Time passes differently when you are seven. I remember watching the photos develop right before my eyes, being able to admire myself within minutes.

My sister Katherine was leaving the next day. She was going away to have surgery, and no one could promise that she would be back. Father Shepherd had organized a special campaign for our family at the parish. They collected toys and money. One man even offered to pilot his small private plane, flying my parents and sister to the hospital three states away. It might be the only time my mother has ever ridden in a plane.

The newspaper even ran a story about Katherine's surgery, along with a photo of all of us, looking happy and shy.

That day—before my parents and my sister left for six weeks—Father Shepherd knelt down in front of me. I saw individual gray strands in his wiry dark hair.

"Be a good girl while your parents are away. Listen to the grown-ups," he said.

I was being sent to stay with my grandfather and his new wife. Father Shep had married them in a private ceremony earlier in the year.

"I can take care of myself," I said, pouting a little.

"You're just a little girl. You must listen to your grandpa and do what he says," he repeated. "Your parents are very worried about Katherine. You mustn't give them any more to worry about."

Father Shepherd had smiled at me and gently hugged me, his breath warm with chocolate and coffee. I was a wild girl and a good

girl. What he said did not make me who I am, or make my grandfather do what he did. He was just a priest in a photo album, and he
was telling me to be a good girl.

That weekend, we three younger children were bundled up and
delivered like orphans on doorsteps. Jeannie—the baby—went to
Uncle Herman's house. She was eighteen months old and cried when
my mother put her down. My aunt wrenched each little finger, one
at a time, from the pant leg to which she clung. My mother often
tells how two months later, my sister had to be torn from my aunt
the same way.

My brother went to his best friend's house. The Darnell family lived several doors down from us, so my brother would pass our
house each day on his walk to school. He would see it blanketed in
snow, unshoveled and white for a whole week before a freezing rain
pocked the drifts with holes and dirt.

I was the last to be dropped off. My parents turned their white
Malibu into a subdivision of small houses on square lots. I had been
to the homes of many friends, but I had never seen a neighborhood
so perfectly laid out. Pots of fake geraniums dotted nearly every
porch. Aging sedans sat in driveways, freshly washed and shined.

I did not see a single child. No bicycles overturned on the side-
walks, left in haste when someone called them in to dinner. No stray
balls rolled into the gutter. My mother turned in her seat and patted
my knee.

"Almost there. Now remember to be polite." She smiled. "We all
have to do our part for Katherine."

This was my grandfather's new house. He had remarried to a
woman with bright red hair and pink fingernails. I met her at the
party on St. Nicholas Day. She brought Jell-O salad in a green
Tupperware dish, and she was not Catholic. My grandfather married her after only three dates. Years later, my mother told me he felt

obligated to do so, because he had sex with her.

Inside the house, my parents did not linger. My baby sister's lengthy drop-off had put them behind schedule, and the pilot, one of the generous church members, was expecting them at the airport. My mother shooed me in the front door and hugged her father briefly.

"She'll be good. I promise," my mother said, looking down at me.

I stood in front of them both, holding a bag of my clothes and tipping my feet toward the outsides of my shoes.

My father handed them a small pile of gifts, so that I had something to open on Christmas day. Regina stuck them in a narrow hall closet. Playing along, I acted like I did not see them.

"We really appreciate this. I can't imagine a worse time of year for something like this," my father said, putting his arm around my mother's shoulders.

She leaned into him. "Tell that to Katherine's heart."

They each bent over and kissed me goodbye. Then they were gone. I ran to the window, watching the car back out of the driveway. I pressed my forehead against the cold glass so I could see them until they turned at the end of the street.

"Well, we were just about to decorate the tree," Regina said. She came and sat down next to me on the sofa. It was flowery and firm.

I looked into the corner and saw a silver tree with twinkling blue lights. It sat on a tabletop.

"You have a real nice one at home."

"We have a real tree. With colored lights," I told her.

My father always insisted we put up the tree on Christmas Eve, but this year it had been up since Thanksgiving.

"Well, I like my little tree. I have lots of ornaments, and I sure could use some help. How about I make us some hot chocolate?"

I nodded my head, though I didn't like chocolate. My mother's words still clung to me. Regina was being nice. I knew my mother did not like her very much, but I couldn't risk upsetting her.

The evening passed quietly. I pretended to sip at my hot chocolate. The blue lights grew brighter as the setting sun darkened the room. Regina let me nibble cookies and cheese cubes for dinner. She played Bing Crosby and Elvis Christmas records, their album covers spread across the floor in front of the open stereo cabinet. My grandfather wandered in and out of the back bedroom, grabbed beers from the fridge, commented on our progress. He took a long swallow and said "Looking good" before heading back to watch TV with the door closed.

When we finished, Regina asked me to help her with the sofa cushions. I handed them to her one at a time, and she piled them in the corner. She heaved at a canvas strap, and a wide bed unfolded from within the sofa. Regina retrieved flowered sheets from the same closet where she had placed my father's little stack of presents. She pulled two pillows from the top shelf, and I shoved them into their pillowcases while she made up the mattress.

Over the sheets, Regina spread a cozy white blanket with rose vines from top to bottom and pink satin binding. I imagined how it would be stretching out alone in the big bed. At home I slept with my sister.

"Nice and snug. How about I leave the tree on?"

I nodded and said, "Mm-hmm."

"Night," she said, turning off the overhead light. She did not try to kiss me.

She rattled around in the kitchen, washing coffee cups and little plates. I heard the hum of running water for a few minutes before she headed back to her own bedroom.

I dug around in my bag for the new yellow nightgown. It was silky, with short sleeves and one button high at the back. When the fabric slid down my bare skin, I felt like a movie star with perfect hair and feathery slippers, like I should lie back and smoke a long, thin cigarette with my legs crossed on the bed.

The blue lights from the tree dotted the wall in the darkened room. Light from the street lamp shined through the curtains. I lay under the rosy blanket feeling the slippery fabric against the sheets. I woke to the hissing sound of his pop top and saw his silhouette in the light of the open refrigerator. I had fallen asleep for what felt like a moment. He came to sit on the edge of the bed while he drank his beer.

When he crawled under the covers and slid my nightgown up, I felt a chill. He took my hand and moved it between my legs. I shuddered and let out a little moan. Startled by the sound, my other hand rushed up to quiet my own mouth.

"Shhh," he said. "Feels good, though, huh?"

Did I control my hand or did he? He was quiet for a while, and then he started to sing.

"Hush little baby, don't say a word."

He rubbed himself against my leg while he sang and rocked under the blankets with me. I kept watching the lights and tried not to think about the good feelings, but it felt too good to ignore. I was seeing colors. Not just the blue lights now but purple and reds. Mostly red. It felt warm, and then hot. Big but good too.

My grandfather cooed, "Good girl. That's my girl."

I don't remember him pulling away from me or saying anything else. That is the sneaky part, remembering the feelings but not the facts.

Proof is what I need. I need my yellow nightgown and the blue lights and angry words and stinging tears. I need a memory of his hand clasped over my mouth, silencing me.

But it was my hand. I silenced myself.

I did not let myself cry out or tell him to stop or pull away or fight.

That night, after he left my bed, I dreamt that I was looking out the living room window. My sister sat outside cutting away at her own skin with a knife. I ran from window to window and always, there she was, pushing the knife down the length of her arm. Her arm was red and bloody, but scientific, like the transparencies in our World Book Encyclopedia at home. I have had that dream for many years.

Nearly every night for six weeks, my grandfather waited until Regina tucked me in. Some nights he only sang. Other times, he pulled back the covers and watched my chest rise and fall. One of the packages left by my father contained new pajamas—pink with little bloomers for bottoms. These my grandfather would push down to my knees.

I remember the strange sensation of being opened up to his eyes. He would just watch me. Most nights he would hum or sing quietly. Waltzing Matilda and Coming Round the Mountain and Chattanooga Choo-Choo were his favorites, and I knew the words to all of them by the time my parents came back.

Every morning Regina woke up first and made coffee for herself, hot chocolate for me. I learned to like it by the time I left. She bought sugary cereal—Count Chocula and Peanut Butter Cap'n Crunch—which I never got at home.

My parents called a couple of times. Neither my parents nor my grandparents could afford lengthy long-distance calls. My mother always asked if I was being a good girl, to which I always answered yes. She would tell me to color pictures and write letters to my sister. I sat at the kitchen table and colored rainbows of red and green and purple and yellow on lengths of hospital paper, the back side marked with skittering up and down EKG lines.

I folded up the long lengths, and Regina helped me put them into manila envelopes which we mailed on Saturdays when we ran errands. I wrote letters telling my sister how much we missed her and couldn't wait for her to come home.

"She is getting better every day," my mother said through the phone.

"When are you coming home?" I would ask, trying not to let my lips quiver on the words.

"Soon."

School ended, and then winter break. Regina took me to school in her car, because they lived too far away for me to ride the bus. At first Regina walked in with me each morning, but finally she just pulled up the circle drive with the other moms and dropped me off. Sometimes I saw my brother, but most days not. The upper grades were in a different hallway.

One night, strong winds knocked out the power lines, so I could not watch my blue lights. We went out to Ponderosa for dinner and when we came home, we saw the streetlights burning bright. Our porch remained dark, however, since he hadn't turned on the outside light before we left. My grandfather fumbled to get the keys in the door.

"Goddamn it."

"Leo, watch your mouth," Regina said, grasping my mittened hand in hers.

"Well, shit. How I am supposed to get the door unlocked if I can't see?"

"Just feel around with your other hand until you find the lock."

I heard the keys jingle. Then he sighed and pushed the door open.

"About damn time," he said, holding the door open for us.

He walked in first. I heard a crack and a thump and then more cursing.

"What the hell is this? A fucking toy store?" he yelled.

Regina and I hustled in behind him. When the power went out, I had been playing with my new toys. My parents gave me a Barbie doll and purple plastic sports car. Regina flipped the light switch, and I saw the car sitting crooked, one wheel broken off. I heard the TV playing in the back bedroom. My grandfather was sitting in the chair clutching his shin.

"Damn thing rolled me right into the table leg," he said.

I reached out to the car, trying not to cry. Regina bent down and put her arm around my shoulders. She lifted me up and took the car from my hands.

"We can get a new one tomorrow, sweetheart," Regina said.

"Why you worried about the damn toy? I'm the one who's hurt," he said.

"Leo, she didn't do it on purpose."

"I'm sorry, Grandpa."

The way he looked at me right then, it was as if I had spoken for the first time. He stared back at me with a hard face.

"Can I get you a drink?" Regina asked. "I put some beer in the fridge this morning. I bet it's still cold."

Without waiting for his answer, she headed toward the kitchen. I waited for the familiar sounds of fridge doors and beer cans, but instead heard the jangle of the wall phone.

Regina spoke into the phone and then called to my grandfather.

"Leo? It's Daniel. Great news. The doctors say she can come home."

My grandfather limped in and grabbed the phone.

"Daniel? —Yes. That's great news. —Where's Gina? —Oh, of course. Well, tell her we said to take care. We'll all be waiting to hear from you." He listened a little longer to my father and then hung up. I had moved closer, waiting my turn to talk to my dad, but no one handed me phone.

He turned to me and put his hand on my head.

"Only a couple more days, kiddo. What we will do without you?" He ruffled my hair.

That was the first night he did not come and sing to me. I waited for him, watching the blue lights twinkle on and off the walls. I missed my other colors. The blue seemed so lonely.

For a long time, I believed that I had been alone all of those nights, lying there touching myself to stop feeling so lonely. I heard myself talking, singing to myself, saying the things he said. Perhaps I did that when he didn't come, missing him and my parents and my own bed.

The next afternoon, Regina came out dressed in a pretty flowered dress and high heels. She carried a large black pocketbook on her arm. I had finished my homework and was playing on the floor with Lincoln Logs. No matter what size house I built, the set never had enough slats for a complete roof.

Regina told me she was going to her bingo night. I could tell she was excited to be going out. She wore perfume and carried a plate of brownies covered with Saran wrap.

"For the bake sale," she said. "But I left a couple for you and your grandpa for after supper. There's also leftover chicken from last night. Think you could get that heated up later for the two of you?"

I nodded.

She hugged me before she left, calling "I'm going now" to the back of the house.

When the sky began to darken, I returned the logs to their silo, pushing the metal cover back on top. I pushed it far into the closet and shut the door.

In the kitchen, I pulled the chicken out of the refrigerator and set it on the counter. I used Regina's little white footstool to reach plates in the upper cabinet. She had taught me how to fill a pan with water and place a Pyrex bowl inside of it. I put several chicken pieces in the dish, along with leftover mashed potatoes. I put a lid on the pan and turned the electric burner on high.

While I waited for the food to heat up, I set the table with plates, forks, knives, and napkins. I got the butter dish from its shelf in the door. I put three pieces of bread on a small plate and set it on the table next to the butter. I poured myself a glass of milk and pulled out a can of beer for him.

When the pan rattled and steam fogged the little kitchen window, I took a potholder and lifted the lid off. Inside, the chicken and potatoes looked wet and steamy. I used tongs to lift the bowl and held it there, dripping water into the pan. Using the potholder, I held the sides and stepped down to walk the hot bowl to the table. I decided to divvy the food onto our plates instead of serving them from the table.

As I was putting a drumstick on my plate, my grandfather came into the kitchen.

"Well, look here at what you have cooked up. Aren't you a perfect little wife?"

I smiled.

He sat down, opened his beer and took a long swallow. Putting the napkin into my lap, I felt grown up, like something I did mattered.

We talked a little but mostly ate in silence. For a long time, that was what I remembered most about those weeks. The silence. I was used to my baby sister crying and my brother playing with Matchbox cars and my mom yelling at the neighbor over the fence, my dad snoring when he fell asleep watching the five o'clock news before dinner. My sick sister was pretty quiet except for David Cassidy music thumping the walls of our shared room. Dinner at our house was always a rowdy affair with laughter, passed food and spilled milk, to eat what was served and compliments from our dad for cleaned plates.

I had never been the only child in a house. Never lived some-where without other children to talk to, fight with.

When dinner was finished, we put our plates in the sink for Re-gina to wash later.

"You know what sounds good to me?"

I shook my head.

"Ice cream. What do you think?"

I nodded in agreement.

My grandfather opened the freezer and pulled out a plastic tub of orange sherbet. He scooped big bowls for each of us. We sat in his back bedroom and watched the football game. He bet me ten dollars to one (which he handed me out of his wallet) that my team would win.

"Which team do I get?" I asked.

"Whichever one you want," he said.

•

When I was sixteen, the phone rang late in the night. It was my grandfather, begging my mother to come pick him up. We hadn't seen or heard from him in years. He said Regina had thrown him out, just like that. Put his clothes in boxes and literally pushed him out the door in his trousers and an undershirt, locking the door behind her. She wouldn't answer the phone, even when my mother tried to call.

My father went to pick him up. The next day, when I came home from school, my parents had moved the furniture around to make a bedroom for him in the back den. A plain twin bed frame was pushed against the wall under a large crucifix, the room's only deco-ration. My mother took him to see a divorce attorney. My grandfa-ther kept his social security, since Regina already collected hers from a previous marriage. The little house had been hers before they married, and so she kept that too. He had not driven for years and had no car of his own.

He moved in with us, offering to sign over his monthly check if my mother bought his beer and cigarettes when she did the grocery shopping. He never left the house except for the occasional doctor visit.

Every Sunday, Father Shepherd came to give him communion. He thrust out his tongue to receive the cleansing host. In the afternoon, he and I watched football games or golf—whatever sport happened to be playing—on the only TV in the house. He still bet me ten to one. I usually won.

At night, I lay in my own bed trying to sleep. My baby sister, now eleven, shared the bed with me. I would wake in the night to go to the bathroom or get a drink. On the way back to bed, I would stop outside my grandfather's door. I heard him mumbling, reciting the Our Father and Hail Mary, asking to die, asking to be forgiven. Just take me to be with you, he would say quietly so no one heard but me.

•

Standing beside the casket, my sisters and mother waited behind me to say their goodbyes. My grandfather's stiff fingers had been curled around a rosary. Reaching into my back pocket, I pulled out the crumpled bill I had brought along. I pushed the dollar between his fingers, so that he held it to his chest. I looked into his face, its filled cheeks and rouged lips, no longer waiting for the apology that would never come.

9/12

WITH YOUR TODDLER ON YOUR HIP, you dial 911.

Johnny pulls at the cord with his pudgy baby fingers. This is before cordless phones. To make the call, you had to make your way to the kitchen, baby in one arm, the other clutching your contracting womb. You try not to slip on the water that runs down your leg.

You can't call your husband. No one carries cell phones.

9/11 is not yet a national tragedy. It is the day you went to the hospital one year and one day ago to deliver the baby in your arms. The one in your uterus should not be born for three more months.

"9-1-1. What is your emergency?"

"I'm having my baby."

"Is there someone there who can drive you to the hospital?"

"No. I'm home alone with my daughter and my one-year-old."

"Ma'am, I'm sending an ambulance. Is there a neighbor who can wait with you?"

"No. I'm alone with my babies. It's too soon."

"The ambulance will be there soon," the operator says.

Johnny starts to cry. You shush him as you rock your hips back and forth to calm him and to ease the contraction wrapped around your midsection.

"Stay with me?" you say to the operator.

•

Between contractions, you tell the driver to take you to St. Mary's.

"What about my children?"

The other medic walks next door to see if Mrs. Trapp, the old lady in the wheelchair, can keep them until your mother arrives. She will load them in her car (no one uses car seats) and take them to your sister's house. Your sister is home with her baby, another on the way.

"Ma'am, we could take you to Deaconess. It's right around the corner."

"No. St. Mary's. We're Catholic."

The medic nods. You don't need to tell him that your husband works in maintenance there, and your father in the hospital cafeteria, or that your sister worked there as a nurse before she got pregnant.

In the ambulance, the first medic places an oxygen mask over your face, though you insist you are fine. When the vehicle hits a pothole, your head rises up and the rim of the mask hits you in the face.

You throw up.

Strawberry soda.

Pink vomit runs down your cheek, staining the sheet and your white cotton blouse. The medic removes the mask, wiggles it from the end of the hose and replaces it with a clean one. He returns it to your face.

You wipe your cheek on your collar.

•

The admitting nurse recognizes your name and says to the attendant, "This is Vinnie's wife. Someone call down and tell him that his wife just came in."

Ten minutes later, your husband jogs into the room, keys jangling from the belt loop of his steel-gray uniform pants. His shirt bears a white embroidered patch with his name above a pocket holding a pencil, a carpenter's ruler, a tiny screwdriver, and his glasses.

The nurse calls your OB. She comes back and says Dr. Young is not available, Dr. Oswald or Dr. England are on call. You can't remember which one you saw last time.

Vince grabs your hand as you are wheeled up to Labor and Delivery on the fifth floor. He rides with you in the elevator and down a long hallway but then he lets go and you disappear behind double doors. This is the time before fathers are allowed to be in the room when their child is born. You must go in alone.

You don't know yet that you will come out alone.

The nurse hooks you up to an IV. The anesthesiologist arrives. He checks your chart, says hello to the nurses. He slaps another mask on your face.

The last thing you hear is Dr. England (you remember now) charging into the room.

"Your son of a bitch. I haven't even examined her yet."

•

You wake up in the maternity ward. You hear a small cry and pick up your head to look around, find your baby. All you see is white.

The curtain moves. A nurse pokes her head around from behind it. She slides it back enough so that you see the bed next to you, a woman in a pink quilted bed jacket, a baby to her breast. She dabs a rubber-nippled bottle to its lips. The baby has a tuft of hair pulled up with a tiny pink bow. A man sits in a chair, reading the paper. He stubs out a cigarette in the metal ashtray.

The nurse says, "I'm supposed to give you these shots to dry up your milk." She pulls the curtain closed again.

"I want to nurse my baby."

The nurse places one hand on your arm and moves to untie the strings at your back. You grab both her hands. It hurts when you turn to reach for them.

"No, you don't understand. I don't plan to use a bottle."

Dr. England appears from behind the white shroud.

"What is she doing in here with these other mothers?" he demands.

His voice booms, and the baby next to you startles in her mother's arms.

"Get her to a private room. Now."

The nurse scuttles out, comes back with a wheelchair. You assume she is taking you to see your baby. Your breasts ache with tingling. You put your hands to them, push the soft washed cotton of your hospital gown to your nipples. It feels like sandpaper. You crave the wet warm suck of your baby's mouth, the only release for what ails you.

The nurse pushes you down the hall and into an empty room at the end. You see a bed made up with sheets and white woven blanket. The nurse helps you into bed and tucks you in as Dr. England comes in.

"Carolyn, the baby had some problems."

You have not heard him cry. You have not held him. You do not know how long you have been here. Instead of asking about your baby, you say, what day is it?

"It's Tuesday."

You came here yesterday in the ambulance. You remember that. You remember the doctor coming in. You don't remember anything after that.

"The baby died early this morning, Carolyn. Vince named him James."

James Vincent was the name you had picked out for a boy. It was a boy.

A son.

You have a daughter and two sons.

You look at the clock. The hands say ten o'clock. It is still morning. He said James died this morning.

"What time?"

"About six."

Dr. England keeps talking.

"He was born with a membrane over his lungs. It made it hard for him to breathe. And he had an underdeveloped heart. It was just too soon for him to live."

When Vince arrives, he tells you that the nurse named Maggie Hensel called the house to tell him James had died, and that she, a baptized Catholic, had baptized him before he stopped breathing.

You interrupt your story here to tell me that not everyone would do something like that. When you baptize someone, you say, and they don't die, you are responsible for their soul.

You begin to cry.

Vince has to leave, so Sister Imelda comes to sit with you. She cries too.

Later you will learn that she gets called to task for getting too personally involved with a patient. The following year, she does not renew her vows. You remind me that Daughters of Charity renew their vows each year. She leaves the order and returns to her parents' farm in northern Indiana to raise goats and chickens.

•

You cannot get out of bed for several days. You allow the nurse to give you two shots, one in each breast, to dry up the milk. Still it comes, in thick hot tears like sap seeping from a cut in the bark of a maple tree, like sadness that you try to hold in but it continues to bubble up from some secret core inside you.

You tell Vince you want to have a funeral.

He is a member of our family, you say.

He is my son.

Vince agrees. He goes to the funeral home and picks out a tiny white casket with a blue satin lining. He selects a small white gown. All this falls to Vince, because you have not yet been able to get out of bed.

At the viewing, Vince watches the undertaker close the small box and carry it in his arms, too small to require pallbearers, to the hearse. That evening at the hospital, he tells you that he wanted to climb inside and ride with his son to the cemetery. He tells you that your mother took a picture of the casket for you.

You lie in your hospital bed, crying milk tears.

•

Fifty years later, when I ask if you were sad to miss his funeral, you say no.

You say you were the one who wanted it that way.

All this time, I blamed the church. I hated a religion that would bury a woman's child before she could be there to say goodbye, all to save the baby's soul from purgatory, but you tell me this story, and I understand.

•

It is nearly midnight now. You and I have been talking for hours. I stand up.

I want to sleep, but I ask one more question. Have you ever been to his grave?

You say, oh gosh, not for years. He still doesn't have a headstone. Someday, your dad and I want to buy him one.

THE MIRACLE OF CARVILLE

*The biggest disease today is not leprosy or tuberculosis,
but rather the feeling of being unwanted.*
—Mother Teresa

MY AUNT HELEN WAS A FRAIL THING. Had she stepped on the scale she used to weigh the patients at intake, the number would not have topped 100. No one, including Helen herself, expected great things from her.

When she took her first vows at eighteen, Helen changed her name to Sister Laura. Every year after, until she died at the age of eighty-seven, she renewed her vows, serving most of those years, more than any other woman in the order, at the Carville Leprosarium.

•

"What name would you like me to write down for you?"

"My name is Francis Martin," answered the young man sitting in the chair across from her.

Sr. Laura had been intake clerk at Carville for five years, the voice and face that greeted incoming patients, thanks in part to her impeccable typing skills, picked up easily after years at the piano.

Francis, like most patients, left home so quickly that he had few personal belongings. Anything left behind had likely been burned or destroyed. Leprosy invoked a fear in people. Even Laura arrived expecting to be sick soon after, but year after year passed without the slighted symptom. Still, outside these walls, and inside at times, the illness could provoke a mob to burn entire households.

"Many of our new residents like to imagine a whole new persona for themselves. It is a chance to start over."

"You want me to forget my past?"

Sr. Laura laid her hands in her lap. "It's not only for you. I'm sure you love your family and everyone you left behind. Changing your name is a way to protect them too."

Sr. Laura waited a moment for him to process her words.

"You mean so they can't find me?"

"I mean because what I am about to put on this form becomes a matter of public record, which means it can be seen by school boards, banks, employers, anyone with a reason to ensure someone's future good health."

Francis looked at her. She could sense that he held her gaze as a way to prove that he was stronger; he would not be defeated by this disease, and certainly not by this tiny woman.

She was patient.

"Daniel. Daniel Lawrence." His brothers' names, he told her.

•

When Sr. Laura was not working in the front office, she was studying, learning pharmacology, and though she did not know it yet, she would become head pharmacist at Carville, an important job in the years ahead, as patients began to receive medication that would allow them, for the first time in history, to leave the leprosarium and return to the outside world with the names they had chosen for themselves on the first day. In this way, Sr. Laura's own hand wrote the beginning and, for some, the end of their story at Carville.

Others would never leave. They chose to marry and have children and live full lives on the grounds of Carville even after their health improved.

None of them forgot the tiny woman who greeted them upon their arrival.

•

Sister Laura grew older. Her hair grayed beneath her white veil. The hope she gave her patients of returning to some version of their former lives was not a hope she held for herself. In all her years here, she had only ever missed one thing: music.

•

As much as Sister Laura loved music, her older sister had been the talented one..

Sister Rosemary, who taught music class, had been raised in a wealthy family with a house on the riverfront. Her vows required that she give all her worldly possessions to the order, including her precious piano. While the instrument no longer belonged to her, she still knew the fingerings and could read music. She provided lessons after school to students whose own families could not provide such a privilege.

Sister Laura's dead sister had been Rosemary's favorite student, who could play any instrument put in her hands. She was good at piano. She excelled at violin.

All of them were stunned by the drowning. The kids had only been a few feet from shore, but the storm pulled them too far out and dumped them from the boat into the river. Her sister's deft hands were useless against the strong current that pulled her under.

As a girl, Sr. Laura had received piano instruction as well. She pounded out sonatas and hymns during children's mass. Her parents and the nuns agreed that she did not have the stamina to pursue a musical education to a higher level, as her sister might. Her mother hoped she might at least give her younger daughter a useful skill that could provide a source of income, in case someday her husband died or abandoned his family, as men are prone to do.

At seventeen, Sr. Laura entered the Order of the Daughters of Charity.

•

Life at Carville left her little time for trivial pursuits. The former plantation, while greatly improved from the early days of the leprosarium, was not a luxurious place to live. The once dilapidated mansion now housed the hospital; patient quarters were built on the sites of former slave cabins. Barbed-wire fencing surrounded the whole place. While water moccasins no longer snaked up the bedposts, as in the early days, plagues of mosquitos still swarmed her when she stepped outside.

Sr. Laura worked and studied, prayed, attended mass and occasionally funerals for those who did most of their living on the grounds before they died there.

Over the years, Carville became a small town, with its own newspaper, a café, even a beauty shop. Many of the patients brought these skills with them.

It was the children who struggled. There was a school, but what was the point of learning about the world when one's own world was limited to the few hundred acres on which Carville stood? One might never see an ocean or walk down a city street. The children grew tired of words; they wanted to see real places, rivers and countries that they knew only on maps. Slowly, as happens for children, their memories of a former life faded. The years spent with leprosy outnumbered the years without. Seeds that would never sail on the wind.

These children haunted Sr. Laura.

Years without their families, sleeping on a ward with forty other boys and girls.

Each day progressed from dorm to dining hall to classroom, day after day, year after year. No birthday parties or new shoes for the first day of school, no evenings spent sprawled on a living room rug. All the regular rituals of growing up cast aside with their birth names.

What could she offer these children? What had helped her?

Music.

Music was a real thing they could make. She petitioned for a piano. Then she prayed. She waited. It arrived on the barge. She enlisted several of the male patients to help her haul it from the river to the chapel. The men kept asking if it was real, it was so light under their fingertips. Perhaps it was only a shell of an instrument, without the guts needed to make sounds.   When the men set it down, though, and she opened the lid, her fingers found the keys.

Notes echoed through the chapel.

Laura posted a schedule and the children signed up, just one or two girls at first, but then more, even some of the boys, encouraged by the teachers and then the doctors, who began to see startling changes in the children who studied piano with Sr. Laura on Wednesday afternoons in the front parlor of the old plantation house. The stiffness left their hands. Their fingers stayed straighter, stopped melting away, the delicate bones no longer reabsorbed into their bodies.

Soon Laura was teaching all the children, as part of their regular treatment routines. And though no one ever did a scientific study or compared children who took lessons to those who did not (for who would withhold such a thing in a place with so little hope and so few pleasures), the teachers and doctors all believed in the Miracle of Carville.

•

"Hello." A nun, small and frail, white hair slipping from beneath her cap, lowered herself into the wooden chair beside Jennifer.

Jennifer looked at her, said nothing.

"You must be Jennifer."

"What are you? Omnipotent?" The girl flipped her long hair back over one shoulder.

"I have a niece about your age, but she has curly hair, like her father." Sr. Laura was smiling. "What she wouldn't give for hair like yours. Her mom sends me school pictures every year."

Jennifer had known girls like that, girls who wanted to be like her.

"Tell her to stop sticking her fingers in electrical outlets. That ought to help."

"I'll be sure to pass along your advice." She put out her hand. "I'm Sister Laura."

Jennifer didn't want anyone to touch her. She kept her hands folded in her lap, but the nun reached over and laid her small wrinkled one on top of them. They were like her grandmother's hands, soft and papery, but stronger, folding themselves around her long fingers and gripping them, getting Jennifer's attention.

"You play an instrument."

Just like that, knowing, not asking.

"How do you know?"

"I know this callus. My sister played violin."

"Someone here plays the violin?" Jennifer couldn't help herself. She missed her music.

"No, my oldest sister, from childhood. She died very young, but she played beautiful music, string music I called it then. I was little, the baby, but she would play for me, in our bedroom, where no one else could hear."

"Oh. How did she die?"

"She drowned. In a river."

"I'm sorry."

"So what do you play?"

"I *played* the violin."

"You don't have to give up your music."

"You don't understand. I didn't just play for fun." Jennifer's eyes teared up. "Everything has changed. I didn't even get to bring my violin with me."

Her parents thought it was too valuable. It would be ruined, or stolen, they said. Better to let them hold onto it.

Sr. Laura sighed, not a sigh of understanding, but a sigh of agreement.

"And now all you are is a patient with leprosy?" Sr. Laura said. "When you know what you were supposed to do with your life, it doesn't matter where you are."

Jennifer nodded, to keep from crying.

"We are two lonely people," Sr. Laura said.

"How could you be lonely?"

"I too have lost my purpose." And now, as if they had both forgotten how close they were, Sr. Laura pulled her hands back into her own lap, picked up the rosary that hung around her neck, fingered it between her thumb and index finger. "I am too old to run the pharmacy, so they sent us someone younger, a man who has a degree from somewhere out east. And with my arthritis, I can no longer teach. They tell me I am free to rest my tired hands."

"So you just hand over your keys, just like that? I suppose this is where you tell me that it is all God's plan and we must have faith that God has something in mind for each of us. That's bullshit."

"You're right. It is. It wasn't easy for me to walk away. But I am getting tired. I wasn't much older than you are when I came here, and look at me now. I'm old. I was never good at math, but I can up add up the years."

"Me either—good at math, I mean. I studied music. And if it weren't for some nosy piano teacher, I would be packing for a trip to Europe instead of sitting here."

"Piano? Well, now there's something else I was not very good at, not for lack of trying, I'll tell you. My mother had a hard time letting go of her dream, especially after my sister died. She wanted so much for one of her children to be a musician."

Jennifer couldn't help but smile. She had begun studying piano when she was four. It wasn't a choice. It just was. She remembered more about her first piano instructor than she did her kindergarten teacher. She had to beg to be allowed to play violin, and her mother agreed only as long as she kept up with both instruments.

"You know, we have a piano in the chapel. I'm sure it isn't what you are accustomed to, but It has been quite a long time since that piano had a friend."

Jennifer looked down at her folded hands, the quiet fingers, so unlike the pictures she looked up in the encyclopedia at home, before her mother ripped them out, fingers like an alien's. How long before hers looked like that, she wondered. She had threatened to quit music a hundred times, to get back at her parents when they grounded her for the weekend before a big recital, but now, faced with the prospect of never playing music again, she felt sick. A whimper escaped from her throat.

"They have lots of treatments these days, you know? Things we could never have imagined when I was young nun, and Dr. Trautman, the head of the hospital, he's a good man, with new ideas and plans for you and all the patients here."

The door of the patient intake office opened. A young nun poked her head out.

"Jennifer?"

Patients didn't change their names anymore. Neither did nuns. This woman wore a badge that read Sr. Pat. She motioned Jennifer inside her office.

"Why don't you come in?"

•

One day, early in April of 1983, an orderly wheeled Sr. Laura into the library. She would be leaving soon, as soon as she was well enough to be moved.

She had lived and worked at Carville for sixty-two years. This was home. But the last stroke left her unable to walk or use her hands, which rested in her lap, curled up on themselves as if they were holding each other. The physical therapists, familiar with patients who had lost the use of their extremities, sat with her every day, working the joints, unfurling each finger. Laura tried to resist, not because of the pain. In her deteriorated state, she still knew there were other patients who needed help. But with Laura trapped inside her old body that refused to do her bidding, the therapists carried on anyway.

Today the therapist was taking Sr. Laura to the chapel to try something. She would not be licensed to practice therapy at any other institution. She began working as an assistant because of her strong fingers. Sr. Laura did not appear to remember Jennifer; she had lost some memory over the years, worn spots in the fabric of her mind.

"We're going to try something new today," Jennifer said, leaning down to put the brakes on the wheelchair. She still wore her hair long, darker now like the bark of a tree, and pulled back into a sleek ponytail that slipped over her shoulder when she bent down. She flipped it back when she stood back up.

Jennifer pushed the chair up to the black and white keys; Sr. Laura's hands remained in her lap. She still wore her white habit.

It had taken a long time for Jennifer to join Sr. Laura's band of musicians. She had watched Sr. Laura for months. The nun did not notice her when she was engaged with the younger students, her hands moving back and forth, playing scales. When Jennifer wasn't observing the old nun, she was reading or writing letters to friends. Eventually, when no one wrote back, she stopped writing too.

That was when she had begun to notice the stiffness in her hands.

At first, she set her alarm clock and came down to the parlor very early, before the sun was up, to play. She would hold down the damper pedal and just brush the keys, playing the pieces she knew by heart. She would forget herself, let up the pressure of her foot on the pedal, focused on the movement of her hands, needing to hear the music.

Her fingers limbered up. She told the doctor, who noticed too and told the therapists. None of them had known she played. Her secret exposed, she arrived at her session one day, and the therapist said she had a heavy load and could Jennifer share the piano with another patient, a slight little girl who didn't even take up half the bench. She tapped out Mary Had a Little Lamb, so softly and so many times, that Jennifer, to ease her own nerves, started to teach the twig of a girl something else. By the end of the week, the two were playing Chopsticks with no mistakes, if a little slowly. The next week, the therapist asked if another child could join her. A month later, Jennifer realized she had been tricked.

By then, she didn't care. She and the children played every day, except Sundays when some of the families came from New Orleans to visit. On Sundays, Jennifer played alone. At her request, Jennifer's mother started to send sheet music: pop songs, things she never would have been allowed to play before, music she would have thought below her talent, but which now made her happy. She played "The Sting," "Bridge Over Troubled Water," and "Tomorrow."

On Monday, she returned to her duets.

When her first student left Carville, returning home to New Orleans, Jennifer realized she could probably leave too. She imagined what it would be like. She had lost touch with her childhood friends. High school friends were teaching at conservatories around the world, playing in concert halls, or less successfully, teaching high school music. Her parents had sold the house and moved into a condo, so Jennifer stayed on at Carville, working to earn her keep, and eventually earning her own paycheck. And now she found herself sitting beside an old nun in a wheelchair, fingers folded around the same tarnished rosary she had worn the day they had met.

Jennifer picked up Sr. Laura's right hand, then the left, as if they were attached to marionette strings. The room was full of people, none of them noticing two women at a quiet piano. Jennifer lifted the rosary chain over Sr. Laura's head. Slumped over, the nun appeared to be bowing to help remove it.

Jennifer placed her right hand on the keys. She moved as close as she could to the metal chair, turning her body to close the gap between them. The older woman smelled of soap. She lifted Sr. Laura's hand and placed it on top of her own, twining the rosary beads around them, securing the two together, the older hand worn and velvety like a leaf plucked from lamb's ear in the garden. The cool keys beneath her, the nun's hands resting above, Jennifer began to play, slowly, moving her hand down the keys to practice her scales.

CROSS MY HEART

THIS IS WHAT I CAN REMEMBER.

I was five when she and my parents flew to Mayo Clinic in a tiny single-engine plane. I stayed with relatives for six weeks, where I was allowed to eat Boo-Berry cereal with blue marshmallows for breakfast. I slept in a twin bed in my cousin Tina's room. My brother and my baby sister went to other houses. We didn't see each other until my parents came home.

Back then, the doctors only knew about the defect in her heart. A tiny cross of negative space where the chamber walls should have joined together. A hole in what should have been whole, old blood mixing with the new oxygen-filled blood.

It made her tired.

So tired.

All the time tired.

She got tired walking the three blocks to school. She would stop at the house of Mrs. Glass. Her son was an actor on television. Mrs. Glass would let her rest there until her lips changed from blue to pink.

We celebrated Christmas early that year, because no one knew if she would come back alive. The priest said mass in our living room, a coffee table for an altar. We ate lasagna and opened our presents from Santa. I received a red gingham dress with a white pinafore.

•

I was six when I began to have my recurring dream. We had moved out of the city to our makeshift farm. In the dream, I am alone inside our house. There is no furniture. I look out the window and see my sister, sitting in the crook of our apple tree. She is carving her skin off with a kitchen knife. It comes off in slices, like thinly shaved roast beef. She does not bleed, but I can see her muscles, red and flexing. I run to another window, but she is there too.

After her surgery, she refused to wear low-cut blouses. She hated the scar, like a pink squirming caterpillar wriggling up her chest. I wanted to touch it. I wanted to know how it felt: spongy, or firm like cooked meat?

When I was older, my mother told me that after her surgery the nurses would come to her hospital room every hour. They would make her sit up in bed. They would tell her to cough ten times, and she cried because it hurt so much.

In high school, I borrowed her white Hang Ten sailor pants without permission. She left for work before the school bus picked me up. The pants had red piping up the legs and three buttons shaped like anchors on each side of a flap that closed across my abdomen.

After school, I hung her pants back up in the closet, hoping she would not know.

•

I was seventeen when she got married. I think she loved someone else. She asked me to be her maid of honor. I said no because I didn't want to wear a dress. I said I would only do it if I could wear a tuxedo. She asked our younger sister instead.

When she went into labor, my mom and dad came to the hospital to be with her. They each stood on opposite sides of the bed and held her hands. The doctor told her that her uterus was divided into two rooms. The baby was in the side that was closed off from the birth canal, the room with no door, no way out. They cut her open and pulled out a baby girl. Her new scar was perpendicular to the caterpillar between her breasts. Now she had two scars, number lines that would never cross, one over her heart and the other over her womb. How did her body get that wrong, leave open what should have been closed and close up what was meant to open?

The year my baby was born, also by C-section, she had another surgery. The doctors dissected her caterpillar. They put new mechanical parts into her heart. The valves click-click when they open and close. She says if you put your ear up to her chest, you can hear the sound of her heart beating. I have never done this, but she tells me this is true.

•

When she got married a second time, I wanted to come. I knew he would be there, the one person I could not see.

One week before the wedding, I went to see the movie *127 Hours*. Just as James Franco's character was about to cut his arm off to save himself, I walked out of the theater. I couldn't breathe. I paced the floor in the lobby, trying to get enough air. I went back in and sat down beside my husband. I tugged on his sleeve and told him I had to leave. He didn't hesitate but got up and left the theater with me. We drove around for an hour, until finally he convinced me that it was safe to go somewhere. We went to a clinic. The doctor gave me a prescription for Xanax.

When we got home, my husband cooked dinner for me. He brought me a glass of wine. I cried and cried, until finally I screamed, "I can't go. I can see him. I can't be in the same room with him."

•

I want so much to tell her that I am sorry for borrowing her favorite pants without permission and for refusing to wear a dress and for missing her wedding. Every time I see her, I say to myself that I am going to tell her why I didn't come. But every time, I feel a wall between us.

Something keeps us apart.

"Do not worry about truth or fiction. Write stories that come to mind. Call them fiction. If they are true, feel free to invent details and dialogue and to round the corners of what really happened to perfect the story. Call it fiction. Tell them you made this stuff up, that you are familiar with the dilemma and problem and emotions of things like this and made the story itself up to capture the emotions, etc. Do not worry about truth or fiction. Just write your stories."

—Phil Deaver, in a letter to the author

SHOW ME

THE COVER HAS A BLACK-AND-WHITE PHOTO of a naked girl and a naked boy. They look a couple of years younger than me. Their legs and hands cover their private parts. Across the top in thick black letters are the words *SHOW ME: A Picture Book of Sex for Children and Parents.*

•

It is Thanksgiving Day in 1976.

The bicentennial. All is freedom and love.

Dinner is over. The kids flee to the living room to watch *A Charlie Brown Thanksgiving* on TV. I am in the back bedroom, playing Barbies with my cousin.

"Julie," my mom calls from the table. "Come in here."

The adults are in the dining room, drinking coffee and smoking cigarettes.

I pull a wedding dress over my doll's naked hips, push her stiff arms through the lacy sleeves and Velcro the fabric closed in back.

"Julie Ann." She calls again, louder but not mad.

I stand up and smooth my skirt around my legs, adjust my white knee socks. The other kids have kicked their shoes into a pile by the door, but my blue leather oxfords are still on. They are attached to braces that run up the sides of my legs, strapped in place by the same sticky fabric that holds Barbie's gown together. I walk through the living room, stepping over and between sprawled legs. The boys lie on their bellies, chins in hands, staring at the screen of our console television. The older girls huddle together on the couch.

"Julie," my mother says again, her arm drawing me to her like a shepherd's hook.

She pulls me in close. "Pull up your skirt and show Aunt Ann your braces."

My dad sits at the head of the table. He is the only one not smoking. He quit when his father died, one month after I was born. He says not a day goes by that he doesn't crave a cigarette.

I look around at the other grownups: my aunt and her husband, my grandfather, and his two sisters visiting from the Sisters of Providence mother house in Terre Haute.

Vatican II has loosened the rules of attire for nuns in the Catholic church. My great-aunts wear black polyester skirts with white cotton blouses and soft crocheted cardigans. Swirls of gray bangs peek out from beneath their veils.

My mother nudges me. "Go on, show her."

I pick up two corners of the hem and lift them as if to curtsy but keep my knees locked. I raise my skirt enough for Aunt Ann to see the gray, plastic-coated metal rods that sprout out of my shoes and run along the outside of my legs.

Mom reaches out her free hand and pushes the fabric of my skirt up higher, past my belly.

"They attach here, around her waist."

I want to cry; I refuse to cry.

I do not look up. I don't want to see their faces looking at me.

My grandfather, who lives with us and bathes me when my parents are out, says to my mother, "Carolyn, let her be. We know what those things look like."

"But Ann's a nurse."

Dad says, "All I know is not one dime is covered by insurance. Not one penny. She's going to wear those damn things every day for the next year."

"Vince, that's enough." My mom doesn't like to talk about money in front of her sister. Aunt Ann and her husband built a new house with a swimming pool and trampoline in the back yard and an extra fridge in the garage for cokes and beer.

I am still holding up my skirt.

My aunt reaches out and runs her hand along the fuzzy black band at my waist. Her fingers are cool on my skin.

"Is this scratchy?"

She looks into my eyes, her fingers still at my waist.

"Sometimes."

"An undershirt might help." She moves her hand away to lift a cigarette from the ashtray to her lips and inhales. "I think I've got some that Kelly doesn't wear. I'll bring them over tomorrow."

The next day, when she drops off a grocery sack full of things, I go straight to the back bedroom to sort through its contents: cotton undershirts printed with tiny rosebuds in yellow, pink, and blue, several pairs of matching underpants. I lift a pink camisole by its thin lacy straps. I don't care that they are secondhand. To me, they are the most beautiful things I own. They give me a new layer of protection underneath my clothes.

•

The following summer, Mom orders a book to teach her children about sex.

My parents belong to a church group called Christian Family Marriage, which the members have nicknamed Cereal, Fruit and Milk. Mom and Dad and the other couples attend weekend marriage retreats, leaving us in the care of my grandfather. They want to be more open with us, they say, and not keep secrets about sex and our bodies like when they were growing up. They don't want us to be ashamed.

She heard about *Show Me* from the other couples. She special orders it. It cost $12.95 plus tax. The day the bookstore calls, we drive to North Park Shopping Center to pick it up. The salesclerk places the plastic-wrapped book into a brown paper sack before handing it to my mother.

When we get home, Mom sits in the middle of the couch. She tells us to sit. The five of us stack ourselves on either side of her.

Mom tears off the plastic wrapping and sets the large white book in her lap. The naked girl looks a couple of years younger than me; the naked boy has long bangs like my brother. My mother opens the book to the first page and reads the letter from the authors.

She turns the page.

Here are the boy and girl from the cover. Both of them have short hair, so I cannot easily tell them apart until page eleven, when the boy opens his legs to show his penis.

So what, says the little girl.

My mother turns the page again.

The little girl leans back to reveal her vagina.

•

I don't go to PE class that year. The black-bottomed shoes attached to my braces scuff the gym floor, so instead I stay in the classroom. My teacher, Ms. Stephenson, enlists my help to teach a young Vietnamese refugee girl to read English.

I cannot remember her name, only her slick black hair, cropped short like my own dark curls, to avoid tangles I imagine.

We sit side by side with a special tape recorder on the table. I feed plastic strips containing pictures into the machine and it reads the sentences to us. The sun shines in the long bank of windows and outside the other children scream and play.

•

When I am fifteen, I run away and stay at my friend Beth's house for two days. Beth's mom comes to sit in the car, where I am hiding, and tells me that I don't want to get in trouble and that going back home will be better than having to go before a judge as a runaway.

Mom and Dad invite Father Temple to our house for a family counseling session. He stands behind our dining table, the one that was turned like an altar. We sit on the wooden chairs facing him. Father Temple tells us that our job as children is to do whatever the adults in the house tell us to do.

I ask, "We should do whatever they tell us to do?"

Father Temple answers, "Yes, the adult is always right."

"What if they tell us to do things that are wrong?"

"It doesn't matter. They are the adults."

•

As if she has forgotten her children are sitting on the couch with her, my mother stops reading *SHOW ME*. She doesn't turn the page. She inhales and lets out a long breath.

She picks up several pages and flips forward to a spread of two teenagers lying on a bare floor. The girl holds his penis between her thumb and forefinger as if she is picking up a grasshopper she found in the grass. Her breasts are like small bowls suctioned to her chest.

My mother flips forward another several pages. Here, two hands, man's hands, grasp his erect penis.

She flips again, very quickly.

A close-up of a vagina, spread apart by a woman's fingers.

We only glimpse this image before my mom closes the book,

which exhales a soft whoosh of air in our faces. Mom pushes herself up off the couch and walks into her bedroom. We hear her open and close the cabinet door above her closet, the one where she keeps private things.

She never gets the book out again.

It's not what she thought it would be like, she tells us.

When my dad comes home from work, she leads him into the bedroom and we hear them talking in hushed tones.

•

At the end of the year, I am permitted to remove my braces.

The doctor tells me to walk down the hall and back. I am naked except for the blue rosebud panties. Then he lifts me up to stand on the exam table. A circle of men surrounds me, pointing with their pencils, taking measurements of the spaces between my ankles, at my knees, and between my thighs. They write the numbers down on their notepads.

Dr. Britt declares, she should continue to develop normally now.

Mom takes me to buy a pair of thong sandals.

At home, I paint my toenails pink.

I've outgrown the undershirts, and the dresses I have worn every day are too short. I replace them with my brother's hand-me-downs: Wranglers from the boys' department at Sears, long-sleeved shirts airbrushed with Mount Rushmore or the American flag.

Soon I add a bra under my T-shirts. Still I refuse to wear dresses.

•

After the birth of my son, I begin to experience anxiety attacks. Once I throw a sippy cup of grape juice against a wall. The lid flies off and purple liquid runs down the white paint. I go to a therapist once a week. We talk about why I feel the urge to pull away any time a man in my family touches me. I want to duck out from under their hand on my shoulder. I tense in hugs. At a family wedding, Uncle Ronnie tells me, you're wound tighter than a bedspring. I laugh it off, but I can still hear those words.

When my grandfather dies, I drive to Evansville for the funeral.

As we walk out of the church, Father Temple says to me, "Well, look who's here. I didn't think you believed in stuff like this." He has his hands clasped around my shoulders, and I cannot get away. I smile and kind of laugh.

It's not until I am in my late thirties, with my second husband seated next to me on the therapist's couch, that the memories begin to return. The memories flash by like flipping through old photographs that have been packed away for a long time.

My grandfather and I sitting close together on a porch swing.

My grandfather and I sharing a cone full of orange sherbet.

Me, at six, with the blankets pushed to the foot of the bed.

Me, touching myself between my legs.

My brother with his hand over my mouth.

Me, in a neighbor boy's clubhouse over his dad's garage.

•

My grandfather moves out of our house, out of the bedroom next to mine, taking with him the crucifix that hangs over his bed. He marries a redheaded woman named Rita because he had to, my mom tells me. She means that he had sex with Rita and by Catholic Law feels obligated to marry her.

Now when my parents go to their Cereal, Fruit and Milk meeting, there is no one to stay with us.

I pull the red kitchen stool up to my parents' closet doors. Standing on the top seat, I can reach the upper cabinets. I open the doors. I can see its white paper jacket. I reach for the book and step down.

I sit on my parents' bed and look through the picture pages.

I see a mouth kissing the tip of a penis.

I see a little boy smiling as he watches the grownups.

I see a photo of the couple taken from above them, the man's body curled about the woman, her legs cupping him, so his butt looks like a heart.

I see his penis entering her vagina, and then on the next page, again, from a different angle, as if I have walked in on two people in their bedroom. The woman's legs are pushed back by the man's hips and his penis is inside her. His testicles dangle like dice from a rear-view mirror. The woman's feet are high up. I can see her soles.

On the next page, the camera zooms in closer. I see the dimpled skin of his scrotum, light filtering through his pubic hairs. It looks like I'm seeing an animal close up instead of part of a human body.

I don't want to see any more, but I cannot stop looking. I flip page after page until I come to the end of the book. I must put it away before my parents come home. I don't want them to find me like this.

·

It is one week before my sister's wedding. I know my brother will be there.

My husband and I go to see the movie *127 Hours*.

Sitting in the dark theater, I begin to have trouble breathing. I tell my husband I have to step out to go to the bathroom. In the lobby, I try to catch my breath. I pace back and forth on the carpet. I go back into the theater and watch the movie. After a couple of minutes, I lean over and tell Mark that something is wrong, I need to leave.

He doesn't ask any questions. He stands up and takes my hand and we walk out.

In the car, he asks me where I want to go. I say, I don't know, I don't know.

Do you want to go home?

No, I don't feel safe there.

Should we go to a hospital?

No, I'll be okay. Can we just drive around for a while?

Of course.

And we do.

He asks me, is there anything you want to do?

I begin to cry and I say, I can't go. I can't go to the wedding. I can't see him.

My husband knows who *he* is. He is my brother.

Then you don't have to go.

I look at him, shocked. I don't have to go?

You don't have to go.

We drive to an immediate care clinic, where a doctor gives me a prescription for Xanax and tells me to make an appointment with my therapist. At home, I curl up on the couch. Mark grills me a steak and brings me a glass of wine. We watch television until I fall asleep.

·

I tell my mother over the phone, with my therapist seated next to me, about the returning memories of my grandfather and my older brother. After the call, I am so tired. Dr. Burt turns off the light and lets me rest on her sofa while she sees her next patient in the room next door.

My mother sends a couple of emails. She tells me that she's glad I didn't tell her about this when I was a child.

Your father probably would have killed your grandfather and ended up in jail, and then you would have grown up without a father.

Finally, after she reads a short story I have written about a little girl molested by her grandfather, she writes to me and apologizes, saying that if she had known she never would have let it go on.

We don't talk about why she bought my grandfather's beer for so many years. We don't talk about why she let him move back in with us when she knew he was an alcoholic. Everything I know has had to be pieced together from my fragmented memories and reading about sexual abuse.

•

My parents are preparing to sell their house. I ask my mom about SHOW ME. Does she still have the book?

Oh, it's somewhere around here, she tells me over the phone.

I imagine it's in that same cabinet over their closet. I could drive to their house, three hours away, and pull up the red stool and find the book, its white cover yellowed with age.

But I don't do that.

I go on the internet and search for the book. I'm shocked to see it listed as a collector's item. But I buy a copy for $125. When it arrives, I carry it into my office and close the door. I sit at my worktable. I open it and read the introduction. In the form of a letter, the authors write that they hope this book will open a dialogue between parents and children, so that kids can grow up in a loving family that does not suppress sexuality.

I can smell the ink.

I turn the page.

Here are the boy and girl from the cover again.

I sit in my office alone turning page after page.

Since childhood, I have been told that my body is not something to be ashamed of, so why do I feel a rush of heat from my belly to the place where my legs meet? I have taken my clothes off when men told me to. Some of them I never saw again. Others faced me every morning across the breakfast table. I have been stared at and touched and ignored. My skin burns any time I feel vulnerable, exposed: while skinny dipping, at doctor's appointments, after sex, when I completely lose myself in the moment and forget how I must look under the camera lens of someone else's eye. Will I ever stop being the little girl whose grandfather tells her to lift up her pajama top and pull down her bottoms so he can look at her? I want to curl up in a tiny ball, hide my face, protect my most private parts from view.

I close the book and hide it under a stack of atlases on the top shelf.

I list *SHOW ME* for sale and find a buyer who pays fifty dollars more than I did.

•

Do you remember the photo of the Vietnamese girl burned in a napalm attack?

Naked, arms flung wide, running toward the camera.

After the photographer snapped the now famous shot, he gathered Kim Phuc in his arms and took her to a hospital where doctors treated her burns. She survived and went on to speak on behalf of other burn victims.

There is another photo of her that most people have not seen. She is a grown woman, a mother now, holding her infant son. Her naked back is turned toward the camera, its ropy scars bared for all to see.

I wonder how her skin endured the stretching and molding of pregnancy. How painful that must have been, a slow pulling as the baby inside grew until it opened her up and entered the world.

Myself, I am nearing fifty. My hair is gray and curls widely around my head. I have weeded out the black and gray clothing from my wardrobe, adopting instead an outrageous mix of patterns and fabrics, bright shoes, a blue bandana printed with flying birds. I ride my daisy-painted bicycle to the farmer's market where a woman stops me to ask if she can take my picture.

ACKNOWLEDGMENTS

I'll begin by thanking the nuns: Sr. Julianna, after whom I am named; Sr. Marie Celeste and Sister Marie Celestine of Sisters of Providence, who visited us as often they could, bringing gifts and smiles and soft cheeks to kiss; Sr. Laura Stricker of Daughters of Charity, whom I never met but was a key figure in the stories of my childhood; Aunt Matilda, also of Daughters of Charity, who gave us pink coconut snowballs when we visited the Motherhouse. These women loom large in my imagination and memories. I was always told that I was the first person in my family to go to college. I believed this until I began researching their lives. These women earned teaching and nursing degrees, master's degrees in music and pharmacology. They touched many lives beyond the city of their births. I wish I had known them while growing up. I imagine that my life might have turned out quite differently.

My therapist says that people are wrong when they say that blood is thicker than water. The true saying, that the blood of the battlefield is thicker than the water of the womb, means we make our own family from those who stand beside us and teach us self-compassion by loving us unconditionally. I am beyond grateful to have a net of golden thread woven by the hands of my sisters-in-life:

Bridgett Jensen, Lia Eastep, and Katy Yocom

Cindy Corpier, Jackie Gorman, and Lori Reisenbichler

Shawndra Miller, Carol Divish and Alyssa Chase

Sena Jeter Naslund, for reminding to always make every word count

Kathleen Driskell, for making sure I stayed

Thank you to Dzanc Books for publishing this collection, to Michelle Dotter for stripping away all the excess layers and letting the stories shine like polished silver, and to Matthew Revert for a beautiful cover design.

Thank you to the Bethany Fiechter at the Indiana State Library and Lyn Martin at Willard Library in Evansville. Librarians are superheroes.

I am grateful for all my teachers and mentors.

I am grateful for all the authors whose books were an oasis for me through many storms.

Thank you to Dan Barden, my first writing teacher, in a community writing class at Butler University, who told me that the writers who make it are not always the most talented. They are the ones who do not quit.

To my family, Mark and Evan and Rachel and Ellie and Alex and Audrey and Scott and Nick, thank for your constant support and love, for tolerating burned meals and late pickups, for not letting me quit, no matter what.